GUNPOINT GROOM

KAMINI KUSUM

REDGRAB books

redgrabbooks.com

RG
books

Published By
Redgrab books Pvt. Ltd.
942, Mutthiganj, Prayagraj, 211003
www.redgrabbooks.com
contact@redgrabbooks.com

First published by Redgrab Books in 2019
Copyright © 2019 Redgrab Books Pvt. Ltd.
Copyright Text © 2019 Kamini Kusum
Printed and bound in India
Cover design and Typeset in Redgrab Books arts

ISBN : 978-93-87390-83-6

For my father
Late Shri S. L. Yadav
with love and memories.

"All, everything that I understand,
I only understand because I love."
— Leo Tolstoy

Contents

CHAPTER 1

Karan walked out of the tattoo studio holding Jia's hand with a pleasant smile playing on his face as he again looked at the name inked on his hand just below the wrist. It read, Jia.

"You are my life, my soul, my everything! And I would keep reiterating it. You know me since our college days. You are the only and the last girl whom I have fallen for. I love you more than anything else and certainly, no one can replace you. And now see, your name is inked on me forever. But it hurts me when you say that I don't think about our marriage." Karan was intensely locked into Jia's gaze as he passionately uttered those words.

Jia's eyes had already turned moist. She knew he meant each word. She couldn't hold back herself and hugged him tightly, ignoring the people around. When it came to love, they had never bothered what others thought of their public display of affection. That's how they were.

"Let's take a walk on the sand," Karan suggested and holding her hand walked towards the beach, inseparable.

"Karan, it's been six years since we passed out and have been in the job. I have turned twenty-eight. My family has been pressing me for marriage for the last couple of years. They have okayed my choice of the groom and are perfectly fine with our marriage. You know that. Now, it's all up to you." Jia stopped and looked at him;

her expressions had the query which Karan had to reply.

"I know everything dear. Nothing is hidden to you. You know how hard I have been trying to convince my parents for the last few years now, especially my mother. You know they have been hunting girls for me like anything. And I have rejected time and again every proposal that they came up with. I have made them crystal clear that I am not going to marry anybody but Jia; doesn't matter if I need to remain a bachelor throughout my life. That's why they have now stopped talking about any marriage proposal. And I believe soon they would accept our love and give their nod." Karan's words oozed out confidence and surety and he meant that. He further continued, "You know how conservative people are at my place- caste, creed, culture; there are a hell lot of things that have clogged their brains making difficult for them to come out of their narrowed and age-old thoughts. But this time, I strongly believe I would be able to convince them. They have already talked to you on the phone and soon things will fall in place for us."

Jia clutched his hand and rested her head on his shoulder. Wrapping his hand around her waist, Karan gently kissed her forehead and they looked on at the waves arising out of the Arabian Sea, hitting the beach and fading away back into the ocean. Everything seemed awesome - they knew it was all the effect of the wonderful thing called love.

It was eight at night. Karan and Jia were still enjoying their time on the beach when Karan's phone rang. It was Sumoy.

"Yeah, we are coming," Karan replied on the phone. "Sumoy and Maya have reached the restaurant. It's a nice one on the beachside. He was saying it serves the best Seafood in the area. Let's go!" Karan informed Jia and they moved towards the restaurant.

"Guys, where were you? Don't tell me you two were on the beach since then! Seriously, somebody should put you on Jupiter and there you would get all the time far away from this madding crowd." Sumoy laughed out as Karan and Jia came inside the restaurant.

"No, No. First, we went to a tattoo studio and then we moved to the beach." Karan pulled a chair for Jia and occupied another beside her.

"Tattoo studio? Jia, you got a tattoo done. Show me?" Maya said in excitement.

"No, no it's not me. I already have one and that's enough for me. It's Karan who got it done." Jia turned towards Karan, a sweet smile playing on her lips.

"Karan, you? Can't believe it? Show that." Sumoy said surprised.

Karan showed then his hand where Jia was inked. "Wow, that's amazing. This small-town boy who abhorred tattoo like anything has got his love inked." Maya said with her eyes wide open and kicking Sumoy's hand through her elbow. "See, this is called love! He knows how to express it and keep his ladylove happy. And then, it's you who hardly bother for my wishes."

Sumoy looked aghast at Maya. "Women will always be women. However hard you try, it's difficult to please them. So, my love for you would be evident and proved only when I ink your name on my body. And you know something; boys do such things only till they are bachelors." Sumoy winked looking at Maya.

Jia laughed out and said, "Maya, Sumoy is right. Guys do such things only till you become a man and wife. After that, who cares? Is that right Karan?" Jia looked at Karan with a smile.

"Don't know about others but not in my case. I will keep doing such crazy things and surprising you lifelong." Came an instant and confident reply from Karan. In the meantime, the waiter had come to take the order. They all settled for Goan delicacies.

"Now, let's come to the question of the decade - when are you two going to tie the knot? Everybody in our friend circle and even our professors are damn curious to know this whenever we get to interact. The entire college knew your love saga. You remember the Romeo Juliet play in our first year of engineering, you two had played the lead roles." Sumoy recollected those college days.

"Yes, and there began our friendship. Later in the second year, I proposed to her." Remembrances of college days brought a twinkle in Karan's eyes. He glanced at Jia, who was already blushing. Karan continued, "No more wait now, this time I am going to make things clear at my home. I hope my parents would agree for our marriage and if they don't, I am going to marry Jia anyways, very soon. I have promised her that this is going to be my last Diwali as a bachelor; next year we would celebrate together." Karan took Jia's hand and held it gently with both his palms. His intense eyes spoke volumes of the love he had for her. Every bit of his word pleased Jia to the core bringing a relaxed and soothing smile on her face. She knew Karan meant that. There wasn't an iota of doubt that he could even revolt his parents to marry her if things didn't shape up the way he wanted.

"You people are goals," Maya said. "And this was a lovely trip just before Diwali. All thanks to Jia for this sudden but wonderful plan. Jia, you are lucky to have your client's office at this beautiful locale. Had it not been for you, we may not have planned this Goa trip."

"I am so happy that my business trip got so pleasant with all of you. But tomorrow you all would be leaving, and I will be left alone here juggling with my client." Jia said with some disappointment.

"Don't tell me that you are spending your Diwali here alone!" Sumoy asked surprised?

"No, no. I will fly to Chandigarh on Diwali. By the afternoon I will be home. The client is working till a day before and I can't leave."

"Maya and I would leave in the afternoon for Delhi. Karan, when do you plan to leave?" Sumoy asked.

"I will come along with you people to the airport. I too have an afternoon flight to Patna." Karan replied.

"Okay. You come back buddy and then we would plan to have a bachelor's party. It's been a long time since I attended one." Sumoy grinned with excitement as Maya frowned at him. "What? Is there anything wrong? You girls are always jealous of our freedom."

"So, we too would plan the bachelorette party, the ultimate one as wild as men do. Hope that doesn't irk you, Sumoy." Maya winked as she teased him.

"Girls are always unnecessarily competing with guys, blindly in almost every damn thing. Now, don't start with those feminist dialogues of some Nari Mukti Morcha and those women empowerment stuff."

"Okay, okay guys. We all would have fun and that's a promise. And hunting the venue would be your job Sumoy; I know you are awesome at planning such things." Karan was grinning seeing his friends so excited for his marriage.

"Don't worry bro! You just get your wedding date fixed. It would be the most awaited wedding," Sumoy assured, happy and excited for his friend.

They all had their dinner and took a taxi to their resort.

"It's so soothing to sit in the lawn under the starry, moonlit sky. And when you have the love of your life just by your side, what else would you need," Jia was passionate in her voice as she intensely looked into Karan's eyes. Karan held her hand, lifted it a bit and placed a soft kiss. "I love you so much, Karan. Let's put an end to this long wait to our love story."

"Dear, I cannot imagine life without you. I have known the meaning of love only because of you and for me, love is synonymous with Jia. If not Jia, then no one else. We could have married long before; you know that. But I waited only for my parents to happily give their blessings. All said and done, I don't want to lose you at any cost. I can't even think of that!" Karan's voice suddenly became grim as he uttered those last few words. He knew well what Jia meant to him. What would he do if her parents got her married somewhere else? No, not at all - he muttered and tightened his grip on her hand.

"Let's have a walk," Jia chirped like a child pulling Karan's hand.

They paced on the concrete pavement on the lawn that shone under the lampposts standing tall on both sides. Walking through the lawn, they came out to the beautiful garden of the resort. The pink roses welcomed them while the fountain seemed to play that perfect romantic tune. The subtle breeze brushed crossed them lifting their mood. Their eyes met, and they found an intoxicating pull in each other's gaze. As they came closer, Karan slid his hands up her bare arms, his eyes fixed on her luscious red lips, partly open, inviting him to plunge into a world of pleasure. He forced his mouth into hers while his hand slipped under her dress only to explore her soft skin beneath her short dress. They knew nobody was around. And even if someone was there, they cared a damn!

They stayed lip locked for minutes until their hands started straying all over each other, their hearts urged for more and their bodies ached for that perfect orgasm. They knew they wanted that. They always did! And it was never in their control. Holding each other's hand, they walked towards their room.

Within minutes, they were locked inside their room. And in another few minutes, their clothes were lying on the ground and the two on their bed clung to each other.

It was midnight and they were exhausted after prolonged lovemaking but still, sleep was away from their eyes. Lying in Karan's arm, Jia muttered, "I don't feel like letting you go."

"Just a few days dear and I will back to you," Karan said caressing her cheek.

"I feel so bad that I won't be able to go to the airport to see you off."

"It's okay. You have an important meeting with your client. I will call you immediately after I land at Patna airport."

"And once you reach home you would be busy with your family forgetting Jia."

"Forget Jia? Not a single day in my life can pass without hearing your voice. You are a dose of drug to me and I am addicted to you sweetheart."

"Yeah, you better be," Jia said with a naughty smile playing in her eyes.

They talked for a while before they slept holding each other.

CHAPTER 2

Karan took his window seat and as he relaxed stretching out, he received a call from his mother.

"Yeah ma, I have boarded the flight. I should reach Patna in the next one and a half hour and then take a train to Arrah." Karan informed his mother.

Soon there was an announcement to switch off the mobile phones. Karan switched his phone off and relaxed closing his eyes. And soon Jia's face reeled before his eyes. Jia looked ravishing today in that formal black pencil skirt and a white shirt. She was to give an important presentation today to her client. If all went well, she could fetch her organisation a deal worth a few crores. Despite a hectic schedule, with loads of official tension, she looked emotional, while seeing him board the taxi to the airport. They would be meeting after almost two weeks. Even this looked like ages for them. Karan was thrown back to the memory lane of his IIT days. The day first he had seen her, he simply couldn't take his eyes off her. She was dressed in a simple white salwar kameez with pink bandhani dupatta, wavy hair let open at the back and those dainty silver earrings adding to her beauty; he had shamelessly stared at her like a street loafer. She had caught him staring at her but just ignored. Perhaps she was habituated to guys staring at her like fools; beauty always catches the eyes of the beholders. He saw her walking towards the girls' hostel. They were all new then in college and he didn't know her that time. And then soon, he had got to know her name- Jia Arora from Chandigarh. Coming from a conservative family of Bihar, he was always shy talking to girls. But his brilliance in studies had landed him in IIT in the very first attempt. He still remembered that day when he went out to the dhaba outside his campus to have his favourite egg paratha when he saw her sitting there with her friends. An instant smile played on his face as he happened to glance at her. Their eyes met and to his pleasant surprise, she too smiled back. He usually went to the dhaba along with his group of friends but today he was alone. He ordered an egg paratha along with a cup of tea. He looked at her again, tilting his face a bit.

She called out, "Karan, come and sit with us."

His heart almost popped out at that invitation. He went and sat with them.

She asked, "How come you are alone today?"

So, she has been noticing him. He felt elated. "My roommate has gone to his local guardian's place for a couple of days while others are busy in the project."

"I couldn't congratulate you that day for winning first prize in the Tech Fest. You have such sound knowledge. Congratulations!"

His heart danced out with joy on that appreciation from her. "Thanks Jia," he grinned.

"You are from Bihar, right?"

Wow! She knew his native state too. It means she had done some research on him. Does that mean she too was interested in him? "Yes, I am from Bihar; Arrah," he answered enthralled. "Have you heard about it?"

"Not exactly. I just know the capital." She smiled and continued, "People from Bihar are usually very studious. I had a couple of friends in my school who were from Bihar and they all were quite sincere regarding their studies."

"Thanks." Karan's heart ballooned with that praise.

That was the day when their friendship started and with every passing day, they came closer to each other. And then he had proposed her when they were about to leave for their homes after their second-year exams. She remained quiet for a moment and then replied looking into his eyes, "I love you too." Those words ran an electrifying sensation throughout his body. And since then they were together. Eight long years had passed since then and certainly, it had been a long courtship. Their relationship never saw a single hiccup. And now, it needed that 'happy ever after' ending called marriage. Thinking of their beautiful togetherness, a soothing smile crept on Karan's face and soon he fell asleep.

Karan was woken up by the announcement as the flight was going to land at the Patna airport.

As he moved towards the exit gate of the airport with his bags, he received a call from his father.

"Yes Papa, I have landed at Patna and just moving out of the airport to get an auto to the railway station. I should reach home on time." He informed.

Karan came out of the airport and looked around for an auto. Just then a young man, perhaps of his age, decently dressed in a shirt and pair of trousers, came to him.

"Are you Karan Rai, son of Sri Jeevan Rai?

"Yes," Karan replied looking surprised at the man. He had never seen him. "Who are you?"

"I am Sunder. Our grandfathers were good friends and my grandpa knows your family well. He had seen you in childhood before we shifted here. When he got to know that you are coming; he wished to meet you. He is there in the car. Could you come and meet him?"

Karan's grandfather had passed away a couple of years back. He knew he was a social man having a lot of good friends even during his old age. Though he didn't know about any such friend who had shifted to Patna but of course, there were many people he wouldn't know or may not remember. "Okay. I will meet him," Karan said thoughtfully and followed the man.

He took him a bit away and pointed at a car, "There he is, sitting inside."

Karan came close to the car. It was a black SUV. Peeping inside, he found a bearded man sitting in the driver's seat, another robust-looking man sitting beside the driver seat and third one at the back seat. Before he could fathom anything, the driver and the man beside him came out of the car and along with Sundar forcefully pushed him inside through the hind door. The man in the hind seat held Karan tightly and gagged his mouth before he could attempt to shout. His hands too were tied with a thick rope. Soon the car was on the main road, running fast as Karan looked aghast. Within minutes of his landing at the airport, unexpected things had happened. What was this? Who are they? And why did they do this to him? He didn't know them. He had never seen them. And there was hardly anybody whom he had grudges with. So, was he kidnapped? He knew a lot of kidnapping cases happened in the area in return of ransom but those were cases of rich businessmen and not a normal salaried engineer like him who had a moderate family background. But then kidnappers too could be of different categories. He had heard of doctors, engineers and lawyers being kidnapped too.

As Karan's mind raced, his phone rang. The man sitting beside him took out the phone from his pocket and switched it off. Karan could guess it could be Jia. He felt helpless and somewhat scared too. What are they going to do to him? By faces, they didn't look like criminals but the way they talked to each other, he could understand they were not much educated.

The car was running through dusty roads and it was now out of Patna. By then, Karan knew the names of other men - Kundan and Raja. All three except the driver who looked older, were perhaps in their twenties.

The car was stopped at the roadside and the driver went out towards the bush to urinate.

"Uncle is calling," Raja said looking at his mobile while still holding Karan tightly by his arm. "Yes uncle, all fine. He is with us. We will soon reach. Are all arrangements done?" Raja replied to the person on the other side and later handed over the phone to Sunder.

"Yes Papa, perhaps there is some network problem in my mobile. The plan is executed well here; now we need to manage there. We will reach home in an hour." Sunder answered.

The car was running again, faster. Karan had tried all means to free himself but all in vain. The cloth was so tightly stuffed into his mouth and hands tied hard that he was neither able to speak anything nor move these hands. By now, what he understood was the kidnappers were a family and he was being taken to their home. But, why are the kidnappers taking him their home? This was peculiar. Was there any feud with his family which he was not aware of? But still, why would they take him home? Karan was perplexed and clueless about what was happening to him.

The car entered the premises of a big three-storey house. Karan noticed the house was decorated with flowers and some lights fixed here and there. There were a group of women and men standing, decked up perhaps for a wedding. They all seemed to be waiting for someone, perhaps him? The door of the car was opened ajar and he was pulled out.

A tall, overpowering middle-aged man with a shapely moustache, in a kurta-pyjama, came to him and scanned him top to bottom.

"He is handsome. A nice match for our daughter." The man said with satisfaction playing on his face and then turning to Sunder, Raja, and Kundan, he continued, "Good job done, boys. Now remove the cloth from his mouth and bring him inside."

Things were now more or less getting clear to Karan. But he was scared to death when he thought why he could have been brought here. "No! It can't happen to me!" – His heart screamed out.

"Why have you brought me here? Leave me." Karan shouted at the top of his voice the moment cloth was removed from his mouth.

He was almost lifted by a few muscular men who forced him inside a room. He was seated on a chair and hands tied behind. The room was bolted from inside. Karan was surrounded by men while the oldest of all, the same overpowering man stood in front of him, smiling mysteriously while his eyes fixed on him.

"Why are you all doing this to me? And what match are you talking about?" Karan questioned, his heart almost sinking with the fear of the unexpected.

"Don't worry son. We are not going to harm you," the man said. "You have to marry our daughter and take your bride along with you."

"What nonsense? And why do you think I would do this?"

The man looked at Sunder, his eyes hinting at something which was received by Sunder.

"Okay, you won't understand like this. Let me make this clear to you in a better way." Sunder took out a revolver from his hip pocket and pointed it at Karan's head on the right. "By now, you have come to know my name. He is my father Virendra Sharma and Kundan and Raja, my cousins. Kavya is my sister and you have been brought here to marry her. Or to say in simpler words- you have been kidnapped for marriage. So, without putting any further pressure on your mind, get ready for the wedding or else you know what wonders a revolver can do!"

Karan's fear had come true. Not even in his rarest dream had he thought that this could happen to him. Groom kidnapping wasn't a new thing here but how could he fall prey to this- how and why? He questioned himself and looked for an answer. He failed to understand. He tried to control the fear that had gripped his mind and looked at the men who seemed to be butchers ready to sacrifice a goat. But how did they know about him, his flight and everything so perfectly planned? Whatever it is, he can't marry. Suddenly, Jia's face reeled before his eyes. And he shuddered within.

"So, you think you would solemnise this marriage at gunpoint. And I am a fool to keep your daughter with me as my wife and would not bother to file a complaint with the police. You are only ruining the girl's life," Karan said with angst mixed hate in his eyes, trying to free his hand off the rope which didn't seem to loosen even a bit.

Karan's words didn't seem to amuse Sunder. He clenched his teeth and tightened his grip on the revolver while the man in kurta-pyjama hinted him to cool down.

"Yes, shoot me," Karan shouted. "Shoot me and look for another groom for the girl. And then shoot him also." Though Karan sounded bold and loud, an unknown fear was constantly haunting him. More than his life, he was worried about his family and of course not in any way wanted to marry that girl. He had a dream of a beautiful life with Jia and he wanted to live that. But somehow, he felt they won't be thinking of killing him.

Virendra Sharma had a smile playing on his face, a twisted and sarcastic one. "Perhaps you don't know us well. Okay, just a brief introduction- I am the right arm to the MLA. Everybody in this area knows who we are and what we can do. In our family, guns are like toys to men. We are not monsters. We are not even goons though some people call us that behind our back. We don't harm anybody unless someone tries to be too smart to us. There had been a couple of murder charges on our family members, but we have got that all settled." The man spoke out with ease looking calm and composed as if it was a cool normal story that had been narrated. He exchanged a smile of pride with Sunder and then with Kundan and Raja. But Karan was certainly not at ease and what he heard now definitely increased his heartbeat. He kept looking at the men and at the same time mulling about his life ahead.

The man pulled a chair and relaxed while Kundan, the macho man who looked more like a bouncer came in front of Karan. "Karan Rai, son of Jeevan Rai, a banker, your mother a housewife and a cunning lady, Parul Rai, your sister doing her graduation - this is your family; right? Don't be surprised. When we tell you the details that mean we keep a tab on all your family members. What time your father goes to the office, when he comes back, which route your sister takes to her college- we have all the information. We have informers everywhere. Now, coming to the point, if you deny this marriage, you don't know what we can do to your family. You all will be finished. And your sister…we will bring her to such a situation that she would remain unmarried throughout her life."

Karan looked aghast at him. His entire world seemed to collapse into a heap of dirt. "Why are you doing this to me? You could have got anybody for your daughter? Why are you spoiling my life?" Karan's voice was shaky while his terror gripped heart sunk into the fear of the unexpected.

Soon, the older man's face hardened, and his looks turned fierce as if he had heard something strictly forbidden or blasphemous. He got up from the chair and came close to Karan. "Spoiling your life? That is a good joke." He paused as he stared at Karan ready to devour him if he spoke anything further. "You people can make a mockery of anybody's esteem; hardly bother about a girl's feeling or what people in the society would talk about her. Just because you are a boy, your parents think they can make a girl's parents spit and lick it. Isn't? You are an engineer, hold a government job and hence a milking cow for your parents; so, your parents would put you up for auction and whoever gives the best price; the deal would be done. And they don't even mind breaking the deal if someone comes up with a yet better price. Even a thief holds some ethics! You people are the worst. But we know how to put things in place. And that's what we are doing."

Karan failed to understand what he was talking about. They knew so much about him and his family but what was this auction and deal he was talking about. "I seriously don't understand what you are talking about," Karan said in a low voice as confusion lingered on his face.

"Don't try to look innocent like a lamb," the man roared.

"Please believe me; I seriously don't understand what all you are talking about."

The man gave a stern look and kept staring at him for a while, trying to read his face. "So, you mean to say your parents haven't informed you anything about your marriage and the girl they have searched for you."

Karan looked blank and utterly shocked. This was a piece of news for him. His parents had found a girl for him and fixed his wedding as well and that too without informing him. He suddenly realised for the last few months, his mother had been talking about her bad health and said time to time that she wanted to see him settled in marriage soon but whenever he talked about Jia, she wouldn't object and simply keep mum. And he thought that she was gradually accepting her as her son's love interest and future daughter-in-law. But he never understood what was wrong with her health. She would do everything as she always did - shopping, celebrating festivals, attending ceremonies, traveling to relatives' places. His mother was tremendously good at getting things done her way, he knew this. And his parents were all planned to get him married to a girl of their choice. But then, if that was the case, why this drama? Why has he been kidnapped? "Believe me; my parents haven't informed me anything about all this," Karan said in a brittle voice trying to gather what could be the reason behind all this.

Silence prevailed among the men as they looked blank at each other and then stared at Karan, who did seem to be ignorant of the whole matter.

Virendra Sharma finally spoke, breaking the silence, "So, your parents have gone down to such level that they have been playing games with their son. We thought that we are the ones been fooled but no, you too are. Fantastic!" The man laughed out loud and then coming back again to a serious mood with stern looks, continued, "Your parents had fixed your marriage with my daughter. They came to our house to see her and handed over five thousand and one rupees to her as their token of blessings. Though we hadn't seen you, we knew through others that you are an IITian, good looking and well settled in a government job and that's all we wanted for our daughter. In our family, my daughter is the only one educated. She holds a master's degree in Hindi literature and has throughout held a first class. We could have married our girl to any business or influential family, but it was my daughter's desire to be away from business and politics and rather get married in a simple and educated family. We agreed to fulfill all your parent's demands or rather I would say dowry- all household goods, a car, and thirty lakh rupees in cash. Form the very beginning, we had understood how moneyhungry your parents are but then we just ignored as we wanted to see our daughter happy. They said that you have left it to your parents to look up a bride for you and their decision would be your decision. We asked for your phone number, but they avoided saying that you are usually busy and don't like to be disturbed. They further assured us that when you come this time, we all can go and meet you and then immediately after, we can have a ring ceremony. We were all happy and satisfied but then, a month later, out of nowhere, your parents backed out of this marriage proposal citing no specific reason. And then, a few months later, we learned they have fixed your marriage with the daughter of a local businessman in their district. That girl had fled away with some lower-class guy and her father had forcefully brought her back after beating the boy black and blue, but this news spread out like fire in the whole community and it got difficult for the businessman to get his daughter married. And then, he found your parents who sold you out in fifty lakhs and fixed your marriage with that girl." The man paused for a while and then roared with a stern face, "Kundan, show him those photos when his parents had come to our place to see Kavya."

Kundan came to Karan with his mobile and scrolled through some pictures. Karan kept looking at those photos, his eyes wide open and heart still not able to believe that his parents could take such a big decision without even informing him. But pictures were saying it all. His parents were giving their blessings to a girl among her family members in this same house. There was no doubt his mother must have been prepared with some superb plan to convince him into the marriage. Karan was quiet, distraught and broken.

He mustered some courage and said in a low voice, "I apologise on my parents' behalf. They did wrong and they shouldn't have done that but please don't punish me for their fault."

"Do you know what mental and emotional trauma we and especially my sister has gone through? How would you realise? You are a boy; you and your parents have the rights to reject a girl anytime, but you would not know how a girl feels when people talk about the whole episode repeatedly." Sundar blurted out in anger.

"Please try to understand. I can't marry…" Karan protested a bit louder this time and said further, "I am in love with someone. We have been in a relationship since our college days and we plan to get married soon. Please don't force me into this loveless marriage which would have no meaning."

Each word uttered by Karan kept adding fuel to fire and for a moment there was angst mixed silence on everybody's faces. This was something they had least expected to hear from him.

Ending the silence, Virendra spoke out strong and loud, "Doesn't matter, still you have to marry my daughter. Nowadays, everybody has an affair before marriage and rarely these affairs culminate in marriages. So, forget your past and look forward to your new beginning. And now, you have seen my daughter in the picture. She is beautiful, tall, fair-complexioned and educated. What else do you want? Kavya even though broken from inside, opposed our plan of kidnapping and forcing you into marriage but we are not the ones who would keep quiet until we settle our score. It's the matter of our prestige."

"I would never accept this wedding. I would go to the police and I would also file for divorce." Karan was strict this time.

The man gazed sarcastically at Karan and said in a composed disposition, "And then we would cut your parents into pieces and throw them away in the Ganges. Nobody would know what happened to them. Kundan has already explained to you well what can be done to your sister. Throwing acid on her could also be a good idea. And lastly, we would see what we would do to you. Go whoever you want to; even police are not going to help you. Police and politicians are our friends. Even your relatives won't come to your support. They all know what your parents have done. Their greed for money has landed you in this position. And one case of dowry could land you and your parents behind bars. Now, don't say anything further and get ready for the wedding. The priest is waiting outside." The man slowly walked out of the room along with a couple of other men.

Karan was shaken and down and out as everything further looked blurred to him.

"Raja, bring the sherwani. We have to get him ready." Sundar said.

Karan's hand was loosened, and he was made to get into the groom's wear.

Karan sat lost and lifeless in the mandap beside the girl he hardly knew and not even remotely interested in knowing but was getting married to. The priest chanted the mantras while Sundar, Kundan, and Raja stood right behind the groom to help him through the rituals as directed by the priest. The wedding photographer kept clicking at different angles throughout the wedding. Any rigidity shown by Karan and Sunder would instantly get his hand over the revolver kept in his pocket.

CHAPTER 3

The wedding was solemnised. Karan and his newly wedded wife were brought to the car that stood at the gate, decorated with flowers. A beautiful heart-shaped placard at the back of the car read- Kavya weds Karan. Karan stood still and grief-stricken by the sudden terrific slap given by his fate. Within a day, his entire world had gone haywire, his dreams of a life with Jia were shattered brutally.

"Now, my daughter Kavya is your wife. Keep her like a precious jewel and bear it in your mind, don't ever let grief come even close to her or you know the consequence. One single droplet of tear in her eyes and you all are gone!" The man said bluntly and then coming close, whispered into his ears, "Don't even dare to think of abandoning her; I need not repeat what I can do!"

The bride was in tears while she clinched her mother tight. "Don't worry Kavya, everything will be fine." Her mother said wiping away her tears.

"Sunder and Kundan will accompany them till Karan's residence. And I have informed Karan's parents about this wedding." The man thundered. His last few words caught everybody's attention, including Karan's who was otherwise standing almost moribund. People looked at the man eagerly to know the reaction of Karan's parents. Karan's eyes were expressionless and torn apart as he too gazed at the man whose every word now made him hold his heart.

"They would give a grand welcome to the bride and the groom," the man cleared the air as faces around smiled. He further said, "They have to." People knew and believed that Virendra Sharma would set everything right. But this left Karan furthermore shocked as he cursed his fate again in his heart.

As the car ran on the road towards Arrah, Karan looked out through the window, distant and still fighting a tough battle within- Why this to him? For what fault of his? Within twenty-four hours everything had changed. What would he tell Jia? How would he live without her? It was just impossible!

Karan was pulled back from his thoughts with the sound of bangles. He avoided looking at the girl sitting beside him, who was now his bride, the unwanted and forced bride. He happened to glance at her fingers locked and placed on her knees. He could feel she too wasn't comfortable as she had taken care to keep a distance from him and not let her any body part touch him even accidentally. Karan was repeatedly cursing his destiny for pushing him onto a road that seemed to take him nowhere. His life was a mess now!

His phone which was given back to him got ringing. Karan reluctantly looked at the screen but name flashing on it froze him to the core. It was Jia! He kept looking at the screen when Sundar said, "Pick up and tell the whole world that you are married now. Put it on speaker."

Karan's fingers trembled as he pressed the receive button, then the speaker and slowly brought the phone close to him.

"Where are you, Karan? I had been trying to reach since you yesterday. Your mobile was switched off. You didn't even call me back." It was Jia sounding a bit annoyed on the other side.

Karan was mum as Sundar stared at him and Kavya too turning slightly, looked at him.

"Karan, are you there?" Jia asked again.

"Yes," he somehow managed to utter the word in a broken and choked voice.

"What happened? Is everything all right?"

Karan was quiet again; words seemed to freeze inside his throat.

"Tell her," Sundar said narrowing his eyes.

"Jia…" Karan struggled to speak but couldn't say more than her name.

"Karan, please speak out. You are scaring me now. Is everything fine at your place?"

Seeing Karan mum, Sundar took away the phone from him. "Namaste. Karan is married and is traveling back home with his bride. He will talk later." Sundar spoke out calmly as others in the car looked at him. Karan's face turned pale and his eyes vividly awestruck at the mere thought of Jia's reaction.

"What?" Jia almost screamed on the other side. "Give the phone to Karan. I want to talk to him"

Ignoring Jia's words, Sundar switched off the phone and kept it with him.

"Please give me my phone. I want to talk to her." Karan almost begged. "Please…"

"Stop it right away! You are married, and your wife is sitting beside you. Just think about her and I need not remind you, again and again, the consequences." Sunder was loud and clear.

"But I need to explain her…"

Sunder looked at him for a while and said, "I don't think marriage is a thing that requires explanation. We all understand its sanctity."

Karan was distraught and numb as he bent down his head. He felt like crying aloud and question almighty - for what sin of mine, fate has slapped me so hard?

Kavya was a silent listener to all the conversation. She gently bent down her head though her face had clear signs of distress and discomfort.

The car stopped in front of a two-storey, white-painted decent looking house. Sunder and Kundan got down from the car and moved towards the gate where Karan's parents and a few other people were standing to welcome the bride and the groom.

Sundar and Kundan stood there for a moment glancing at the house which had been decorated, though it clearly looked like haphazard work and then they went to Karan's parents. With a grin on his face, Sundar said in a voice almost like that of his father, "Good work in a short time. Now maintain this smile and welcome your daughter-in-law. My father has already given you all the preaching and I need not repeat it."

Karan's father nodded instantly with a forcefully induced smile.

Sundar and Kundan left after a while. The bride was taken inside with all the rituals. The faces around however showed no joy of a wedding. Some faces did manage to be normal with some joyful expressions, a few others stared curiously at the bride while Karan's parents had lost the smile they had forcefully tried to maintain when

Sundan and Kundan were there. Karan was mute and immune to what was happening around. Without saying a single word, he mechanically moved towards his room and locked himself.

"Sarita, go and see him." Karan's father said turning to his wife, looking tense and concerned for his son. He could understand what his son would be going through. This unexpected happening had shaken the entire family and the most impacted was Karan whose life had taken a whole new turn.

Sarita rushed towards the room where her son had locked himself. She knocked at the door, but no reply came. She knocked again and then again constantly; still, there wasn't any reply from inside.

"Son, please open the door. It's unfortunate and a shock for all of us too. Please open the door, Karan." Sarita turned teary as she requested. She had never seen her son behave this way earlier. Cheerful and always confident Karan could handle any situations with a smile and if ever things didn't go as per his wish, he would say calmly and relaxed, "Never mind. It happens." But he wasn't the same now rather broken from inside, frustrated and hopeless.

"Mummy, please go and leave me alone. I don't want to talk to anybody." Came a reply from him, the door still shut.

Sarita knew he meant it and she too wasn't sure what she would talk to her son. The situation was such that all were still too traumatised to handle it. Sarita slowly went back to the room where the bride was, surrounded by a bunch of people. After meeting and greeting the bride people gradually left. They knew in what situation the marriage had taken place and it was better to leave the family alone.

Karan's sister Parul who had been curiously looking at her

sister-in-law since she stepped inside the house, came close and sat beside her. Her eyes were fixed on Kavya, almost scanning her.

"Bhabhi is so beautiful. She is well educated and holds a master's degree. What else one wants? I think whatever happened, happened for good." Parul said gravely and then turning towards her mother further continued, "Ma, we have to accept that matches are made in heaven and I think she is the best match my brother can have."

Sarita was quiet for a while and then said, "Kavya must be tired. Don't know when Karan would open the door. Parul, take Kavya to the room beside Karan's. She should take some rest. Later we would arrange her luggage in Karan's room."

Parul led Kavya to the room. "Bhabhi, you can change and take rest. I will bring your meal here."

Kavya nodded and bolted the room from inside. She had been holding her tears back for long. As she sat on the bed a thick stream of tear rolled down her cheek. Her fate had conspired against her throwing her into a situation where her future seemed a blur. She had instantly liked Karan's photo when her father had shown it to her as her prospective groom. It won't be wrong if she thought she had fallen in love with the man in the photo. That smile, that calm disposition, that simplicity- everything about him had captivated her heart. She was in seventh heaven when Karan's parents had come to see her and fixed their marriage.Many times she would be tempted to think about him - how he talked, how he smiled, how he walked. Her imagination even pulled her into the world where they kissed and made love. And now she is married to the same man. She should feel to be the happiest and the luckiest woman but unfortunately, there are just tears left to her fate. She never wanted things to happen this way. She had almost got over the pain of that failed marriage proposal. She had so much opposed her father's plan of abducting Karan. But nobody cared; neither her father nor her brothers. Marriage could be forced but not love-she had argued but they refused saying once married, everything will be fine. She had now known that Karan had a girlfriend whom he loved so much and wanted to marry but she had intruded into his life crushing all his desires. Kavya cried like a child as tears constantly poured down wetting her saree. She heard Parul coming towards the room and wiped her tears with her saree. Hearing the knock on the door, she opened it.

"Bhabhi here is your meal," Parul said as she placed the covered plate of meal on a tool. She turned towards Kavya only to find her eyes red and a few droplets still lying in the corners of her eyes. Even after wiping them, tears had popped out of her eyes again; she had failed to control her emotional outburst.

"Bhabhi, you are crying." Parul sat beside her sister-in-law, looking at her worried. She was quiet for a moment, not knowing what to say. Console her? If yes, for what and how? Kavya was a newly wedded wife and needed wishes and blessings from all but unfortunately, on the very first day at her husband's home which was her home too now, there were tears loaded in her eyes. Parul gently held her hand between her palms and said, "Every girl enters her husband's house with a dream, dream of a blissful life where she is loved and respected by her husband and his family. I don't know whom to blame for this unfortunate situation-my parents, your parents, the fate or all of them. Ultimately sufferers are just two people, the bride, and the groom. Men still can take out their frustrations but for a girl and that too in a new home with new relatives, I can understand how difficult it can be. Bhabhi, I may not voice my opinions before elders or talk much on this situation, but I would always pray that God may fill your life with immense joy and all that you deserve. Now, please have your meal." Parul pulled the tool and gave the plate into Kavya's hand. "I got to go to the kitchen. And don't think much." Parul smiled and moved towards the kitchen.

Though Kavya hadn't had anything for last so many hours, she didn't feel like eating after having a few bites. All she wanted was a shower to relax her mind and put an end to all the negativity that had been flocking her mind since she got married to Karan. She took shower and changed into a light comfortable saree. She agreed to herself that there was no point in mulling over what happened. The fact is that she is now the wife of Karan Rai. Yes, he had a girlfriend whom he wanted to marry but that couldn't happen. It sounds like a common thing that happens in our society. Not every love affair culminates into marriage. But she did realise that things were not that simple as it sounded in her case. For her, it might be a marriage that was arranged but for her husband, it was a forced marriage and as people said here- 'kidnapped wedding'. And the ground reality is she is an unwanted bride; an unwanted wife for Karan. The road ahead was certainly difficult for her, but she had decided she would be giving her best for this marriage to work, leaving the rest into the hands of almighty. She lied down on the bed and soon fell asleep.

CHAPTER 4

Karan came out of his room and glanced over the wall clock as it stuck seven in the evening. His parents had been waiting for him while Parul was sitting with Kavya in another room.

"Son, you haven't eaten anything since morning. Should I bring something for you?" Sarita asked rushing towards her son as she saw him out of his room.

He moved towards the kitchen turning a deaf ear to his mother. He gulped down a glass of water and paced towards his room when his father called, "Karan, come here." He turned and looked at his father who was sitting in the living area. Karan went and quietly stood in front of his father.

"Please sit here. We need to talk."

"You think there is still anything left to talk about," Karan said in a voice devoid of any emotions.

"Son, I know whatever happened is shocking."

"Shocking for you all? Really?" Karan interrupted loud.

"Son, we never knew something like this could happen," Sarita said in a low and meek voice.

"Don't say that. It's all because of you. Your greed has put us all in this situation." Mr. Rai who was usually a calm and soft-spoken man, was loud and harsh today. "I had told you so many times. But you never listened to me and always did what you liked and forced me too to dance to your tunes. I was stupid. My weakness has made me a culprit before my son. We never cared for our son's feelings. First, we fixed his marriage with Kavya without even informing him and then your hunger for more dowry made us fix his marriage with that businessman's daughter who was not even remotely a match to our son; not to forget the fact that she had run away with her boyfriend. Now, this whole mess! I don't blame Kavya's parents; they did what they felt right and all for their daughter."

Sitting in the other room, Parul and Kavya could hear all. Parul quickly came out in the living while Kavya stayed back. Hearing their argumentative discussion, Kavya knew this was to happen. Many more nasty situations she may have to face; she just tried to prepare herself and make her heart strong enough.

"You all played games with me; nothing else and then got trapped in your vicious plot. I was such a fool to think that you are accepting Jia and our love. Shame on you ma! You tried to sell your son and not just once! For you only money is everything; rest your son and his life is of zero importance. I was a cow whom you put to sale in a cattle's market and then sold to the highest bidder. Isn't it?" Karan blurted out in anger without even taking a pause and then looked at his sister, "Parul, you were aware of all this but still you never bothered to inform your brother? You too became a party to this nasty game!"

Parul was mute as her eyes turned moist. Her brother was right. She was aware of what her parents were doing but couldn't come out with the truth to her brother. "Bhai, please forgive me. Mummy had strictly instructed me not to say anything to anyone, especially you. You know, no one in our family can act against her." Parul spoke in a voice that was chocked and down with repentance.

Karan became mum, his heart bleeding with the pain of losing Jia. His mother was already sobbing seeing that angst on her son's face. "You spoiled my life; you killed me. Now forget you have a son." Karan almost shouted, his voice torn apart in grief.

Sarita shivered with an unknown fear of losing her son; her heart sinking to see that hatred on his face. Will her son never come to her? Will he never love and respect her the way he always did?

"Son, don't say that. Punish me any way you want but don't say that. I admit it was entirely my fault. I can't reverse the time and situations now, but I will return whatever money Kavya's parents have forcefully given us yesterday. Son, we just want you to be happy." Sarita almost begged to forgive her.

"How is that going to help me mummy? You have already complicated my life." Karan spoke indifferently of the tears that had flooded his mother's eyes. He paused for a second and then continued, "I want to end this marriage. It's difficult for me to even think of this relationship! And what relationship are we talking about anyway?"

For a moment Karan's parents and his sister looked blank at him. What was going on in his mind? Was he thinking of leaving the girl or what? Mr. Rai couldn't suppress the fear of something unexpected that his son may decide to do. "Karan, please don't even think of leaving her. Whatever be the circumstances, now you are married to her. She is your wife now. However notorious her family background is but she is a nice girl. Please accept her and start a new life with her," Mr. Rai kept gazing at his son in a wait to his response.

"Son, you know what kind of people they are. They can go to any extent if at all this marriage ends. They would harm you, my son…They would kill you." Sarita could barely speak those last few words as her throat was choked.

"I wish they kill me. And then the whole problem would come to an end. But their revenge won't just stop at me. You all will be finished. I don't know what they would do to my sister. They have already made everything crystal clear to me and I know they mean it. They are those uncivilised goons who fear neither law nor police. This isn't a new thing here. But why am I blaming them when my parents couldn't think like civilized elements of this society." Karan's frustration was speaking loud and certainly piercing though his parents' hearts. "What would I tell Jia? How would I live without her?" Karan couldn't just control those droplets that effortlessly burst out of his eyes.

Parul came closer to her brother and wrapping him with her arms, hugged him tightly. "Bhai, please leave everything to time. I know it's easy to say but I strongly feel that God will restore all the happiness to your life. I don't know how and when but for sure."

Kavya was sitting inside the room listening to everything with a heavy heart and moist eyes. Destiny had slapped not just her but Karan too. She strongly felt that fate had perhaps been harder on Karan suddenly putting a wall between him and his ladylove.

CHAPTER 5

It was six in the morning. Though Kavya was already awake for quite some time but had just kept her eyes closed. She didn't want to open her eyes to the harsh reality of her life and go back to the world where suddenly things had changed for her. She was twenty-four and married to a handsome and well-settled man in government service. All that she had always wanted was- to be a housewife, love her husband, his family and get lots of love from all. But not the way things had happened to her. Everything looked so complicated, uncertain! She was married for a week now and her husband hadn't spoken a single word to her. His room was hers now, but he would take a pillow every night and sleep in the other room. She made tea every day in the morning and offered everybody. At first, Karan refused saying, "No, I don't want" though everybody in the house knew he was the first to clamour for the morning tea. But when Mr. Rai insisted, he took the cup without even looking at Kavya. Her in-laws had been good to her. They knew they had done wrong, they realised it and had accepted the decision of destiny. Now, all they wanted was to see their son happy and settled in marriage, accepting Kavya his wife. Kavya had heard them talking to Karan a couple of times, trying to convince him to forget his past and move ahead in life. Forget his love Jia and move ahead- was it possible for him? He will be going back to Gurgaon and then there would be Jia. Kavya was sure he would take her along because of the pressures from both the families and one thing that she had understood by now that he was a family man. He wasn't self-centered, he had those human feelings, he thought about his parents and sister and cared for them. But what would happen when he would face Jia there. They love each other; how is Karan going to handle the situation? What would be his behavior towards her? Kavya thought to herself. This was a big question mark. He hadn't talked a single word to her till now. Going back to Gurgaon, he could perhaps forget there is even a woman to whom he is married. Will he leave her for Jia? Kavya shuddered with fear. But there was no point thinking over this. There was nothing she could do. She had to leave everything to her fate! Kavya pushed away all those haunting thoughts and got up from her bed.

After taking a shower, she draped a yellow silk saree and neatly applied sindoor in her middle-parted hair. She quickly moved towards the kitchen to prepare tea for all.

Taking the tray of tea, she went to her mother-in-law who was watering the plant in the garden at the backside of the house. She was fond of her plants and watered them every day in the morning as a ritual. Kavya offered her a cup of tea.

Sarita took the cup of tea and said with a smile, "Long live daughter. Did Karan get up?"

"He is perhaps in the living room with papa. I will just go and serve them tea." Kavya replied and turned towards the room.

"Kavya, listen daughter." Sarita stopped her.

Kavya turned towards her.

"I know Karan is not talking to you and doesn't even sleep in his room. It's very difficult for a wife to face such reluctance from her husband. But always remember, you are his wife, his life partner; it's a relation that is sacred, closest and lasting forever- till the last breadth. That's how our society takes the institution of marriage. You give your best to this marriage and I hope he too would soon understand this." Sarita was thoughtful, a bit concerned but hopeful as well.

Kavya didn't say anything but just nodded agreeing to her mother-in-law. At her heart, she knew it wasn't going to be easy. She moved towards the living room while Sarita followed her.

Karan was sitting with his father; both flipping through the pages of newspapers. Kavya offered her father-in-law the cup of tea and then she looked at Karan trying to overcome the hesitation she faced every time she was in front of him though he didn't bother to look at her. She offered him tea. He didn't respond. That wasn't unusual. In the last one week, Kavya was habituated to such behaviour.

"Kavya, keep it on the table. You too have your tea and wake up Parul. She is sleeping like Kumbhkaran. You can only wake her up. She listens to you." Sarita said sitting on the sofa beside her husband.

Kavya nodded and keeping Karan's cup of tea on the table, went towards Parul's room. She knocked at the door. It was already open as usual. Kavya went inside and kept the tray on the table beside the bed. She gently shook Parul's arm, "Parul, get up and have your tea. You would get late for your college."

Parul struggled to open her eyes. "Get up," Kavya said affectionately.

"Good morning bhabhi," Parul got up and sat putting the pillow behind her back. "You are looking so beautiful. Seriously, a fairy!"

Kavya smiled looking at her. Parul was a few years younger to her and in the last one week, she had become closest to her among all family members. Though she was her sister-in-law, Kavya felt she was no less than a sister to her, always ready to help her. The situation wasn't that bad as she had thought it would be when getting married. Everybody had now accepted the fate and heartily accepted her too in the family; except her husband. And for her, that was perhaps the biggest concern.

Sipping tea and keenly observing Kavya's changing facial expressions, Parul said, "Bhabhi, I know what's going on in your mind. But, please don't think much. Thinking and sinking your heart anticipating the future isn't going to help; it would rather put you to depression. Believe me, all is going to be well."

Parul was always so supportive. Kavya just wished her words turned true. She nodded and said, "Now, get up or you would miss your first lecture."

Jeevan and Sarita were seated at the dining table while Parul came switching off the TV. She had been watching her favourite serial which she usually did in the evening. She had cut the vegetables in the kitchen and took the flour out to knead it but on Kavya's repeated insistence, she left the kitchen to watch her show. Parul was always ready to assist Kavya. Though Sarita didn't want the new bride to be involved in domestic chores so soon but Kavya had requested her, "Mummy, please let me cook. I just love cooking and I used to do everything at parents' home. Now it's my home. So, let me do it." For a while, Sarita felt guilty for all the wrongs she had done but everything aside, Kavya was an ideal girl that every family would look forward to welcoming.

Kavya served the plates with bowls. Karan hadn't yet joined. She looked at Karan who was sitting a bit away, engrossed in his laptop. He had been checking and replying to his official mails. Kavya just couldn't dare to call him. Understanding Kavya's predicament, Mr. Rai called out, "Karan, come join us. You can do that later."

"Papa, I will join in a few minutes. There is an urgent mail from my boss that I had missed. Need to provide some information."

Kavya served all and just stood there waiting for Karan. "Kavya, sit and have dinner," said Sarita. Sarita always cared not to let Kavya feel left out in any circumstance.

Kavya pulled a chair and sat down to have dinner along with all. Within a few minutes, Karan too came and stood near the dining table for a moment looking at the vacant chair beside Kavya. He didn't want to sit beside her but seeing no other option, reluctantly pulled it to sit. Seeing him join the table, Kavya immediately got up and picked up the bowl of curry to serve him.

"I will do it myself," Karan said strictly without even looking at her.

Hearing this, Kavya's legs froze for a moment.

"What's the harm if she serves you? Will the food turn into poison? She has served all of us." Karan's father said staring at him.

"How would the food matter when the whole life is poisoned?" Karan said in a low but firm voice, looking straight at his father.

There was silence in the room. His words merely expressed what he was going through and even though he never expressed his angst in words except for the first day, it was very clear that the whole incident had jolted him to the core and scars weren't easy to be healed. Kavya kept the bowl back at the table and went to her chair quietly. Karan served himself and then no one said anything further. Kavya felt like a big stone had been thrown with force at her brittle heart, breaking it into pieces… She just hoped of things getting better!

Kavya made the bed and arranged the pillows. She knew Karan would anyway not sleep in the room but once or twice a day he came to the room, to take either a book, a file or any other thing he required from his cupboard or the shelf and then to keep them back if required. While he came into the room and took his things, he would ignore her presence. Today Karan hadn't come to collect any of his things; perhaps he didn't require. Just then Kavya saw him through the window. He was talking on the phone walking briskly, tense. Then she heard the name, Jia. And then rest there was nothing she could think of. Jia was his girlfriend, they had been in love; this marriage can't put a sudden and quick end to their feelings. And why at all would the feelings die just because of this loveless and forced marriage? And despite all the hopes given by her in-laws and parents, she still had a fear if at all her husband would give her a place in his life or, in true sense they would be a husband and wife ever.

CHAPTER 6

Parul was assisting Kavya to pack her bag, while Sunder and Kundan were sitting in the living room with Karan's parents. Karan too was there but almost like a dummy that had been forced to sit.

"I think these are enough. Anyway, you would be coming back after two days and would leave for Gurgaon." Parul said looking at the trolley containing Kavya's stuff.

"Yeah, you are right," said Kavya though the thought of going to Gurgaon along with her husband with nobody else with them, sent out a sensation across her body. She froze for a moment but then got back to herself hearing her mother-in-law call her out. "Kavya, are you ready?"

"Yeah, I am ready. Just coming." Kavya replied and quickly zipped the trolley.

"Have a nice journey bhabhi and enjoy your stay with your parents," Parul smiled and hugged Kavya.

Kavya had always heard not-so-pleasant stories about sisters-in-law but Parul was different; a sister, a friend and big anchor to her in this house.

Kavya came out with the trolley and her brothers, Sunder and Kundan got up to leave. "We are glad to see that our sister didn't have any problem or complaint during her stay here. That's good.

And I hope in future too you all would keep her happy." Sundar said in his trademark dominating voice, akin to his father. And then turning to Karan, he continued with raised eyebrows, "Why is Karanji so quiet? Has he still not realised and accepted that he is now a married man; married to our sister?"

Karan looked at him and wanted to shout out loud but could just give a dry look at the brothers. His father instead tried to handle them, "Everything is fine Sundar. We have already let bygones be bygones and now Kavya is a member of our family. Moreover, she is a sweet girl and very well behaved. Whatever had been the circumstances, now we all have to move on."

"That's good to hear," Sunder said nodding his head and then giving a cold look to Karan, moved towards the car holding Kavya's trolley.

Kavya touched the feet of Karan's parents and looked at Karan who was standing expressionless and completely overlooked her.

Kavya got into the car at the back seat and soon the car moved towards the exit gate. Kavya turned back, her eyes looking out for Karan but perhaps he had already retired into his room.

"Hope they are treating you well." Kavya's mother asked making her sit and feel relaxed. All the family members including the relatives living nearby had dropped in to meet her and surrounded her staring curiously at her as if she was to give some breaking news or narrate some spicy saas-bahu saga or some entertaining in-laws Puranas.

"Did they ever talk about the incident or tell anything to you?" Her father asked shrinking his eyebrows and almost ready to attack them if he heard anything wrong.

In the meantime, Kavya's aunt came with a glass of water for her. Even before Kavya had finished the glass of water, her aunt simply couldn't control the volley of questions erupting in her mind, "Your mother-in-law is no less than a vixen. That's what I could understand when I last met her. Does she make you do domestic chores? I hope she doesn't pass any absurd comment. And what about Parul? She too seems a replica of her mother."

"Aunty, it's nothing like that. I don't know what and how mummyji had been or what you understood, but she is nice to me and always supportive. They all believe and respect the sanctity of marriage and treat me well. And Parul is such a sweet girl; always ready to help me. No doubt, it's a nice family." Kavya said, silencing her aunt and everybody else who had queries ready to bombard her.

"Whatever you say Kavya, but we all know that Saritaji is responsible for all that happened," said Kavya's mother not willing to give up accusing them.

"She has realised her fault. It's always good to bury the past and move on. And that's what everybody is doing. So, let's not discuss or ponder on it anymore." Kavya said firmly.

Sunder who was quietly listening till now, questioned with a stern look, "And what about Karan? I didn't see even a dash of a smile on his face all this while I was there. Ultimately, you two have to live together."

"That, you all should have thought before kidnapping him and forcing him into marriage. Of course, you can't expect a smile on his face. He loves a girl whom he had wanted to marry; he had some dreams which all have collapsed. Whoever's fault it was, he was certainly nowhere into all this and was completely innocent." Kavya spoke out a bit loud this time, unusual of her. All looked at her with a surprised expression. They had never seen her reply to her elder brother this way. Usually a meek and gullible Kavya had hit out hard on all.

"Don't give us Kavya the preaching of what is right and what is wrong. We have some prestige, some respect in society and are no fools. Above all, we care for you." Sunder wasn't going to keep silent.

"Okay, you all did what was right according to you and decided and declared my future. Now, please understand, this is my life and let me live it and handle it my way. Karan is a nice man, soft-spoken, well behaved and understands human emotions. But you shouldn't always force things on good people like him. I respect him and believe that we should leave things to time. Now, I am not interested in discussing my husband or his family." Kavya made it amply clear, shutting everybody especially the ladies of the neighbourhood who had been murmuring and waiting for their turn to poke her with their saucy questions that could only offend her.

"Now, don't force me to go there," Karan said, irritated looking away from his mother. "At times, I doubt you are my parents."

"Son, I understand your emotions and we have already talked a lot on this. But it's a tradition and you have to go to her home to bring her back."

"You people have already planned to send her along with me to Gurgaon. Now, is it necessary to go to her house? I don't want to face those men again. Those are arrogant goons!"

"Okay, they are goons. But Kavya is a sweet girl and not like her family members. Moreover, they aren't going to harm you. And what do you mean we have planned to send her along with you. She is your wife, your better half and will accompany you like your shadow lifelong. So, go and bring her back and papa is also going along with you." Sarita made it clear to Karan.

Karan simply gave up. There was no point arguing anymore.

Karan and his father received a warm welcome at Kavya's home. Virendra Sharma, the head of the family had strictly instructed all especially the boys Sunder, Kundan and Raja who lost their tempers now and then that forgetting everything else, father and son should be treated well. After all, they are now their daughter's family. All this while their stay at Kavya's place, Karan hardly spoke anything although his father at times whispered him to at least maintain a decent mood to which Karan would just fake a smile.

Kavya's heart was all smiles all along the way back to her in-laws; after all, Karan had come to bring her back home. Though he didn't say anything to her, at least he came and that was enough to enthrall her. A day after tomorrow she would be leaving for Gurgaon with her husband and a lot of random and mixed thoughts kept repeatedly bouncing in her mind.

Kavya was preparing breakfast in the kitchen while Sarita and Parul were busy preparing mathri.

Karan loved it and would always ask his mother to pack a lot of mathri for him. This time he didn't say even once. But Sarita didn't fail to pack all his favourite things - thekua, shakarpara, jackfruit pickle, and a few more things.

Sarita looked at Karan who was busy doing his push-ups. Karan was very particular about his exercise. No matter what was happening in his life, this was one thing that helped him release his stress.

"Karan, tomorrow Kavya and you would be leaving. Take her to market for shopping. Buy her some nice suits from branded showrooms and whatever other things she requires. In Delhi and surrounding areas, girls hardly wear saree which comes out of wardrobe only on some occasions." Sarita said while Karan wiped his face with towel finishing his exercise, but he didn't reply. Instead, he moved to the washroom.

Seeing him say nothing, Sarita said again, "Karan, did you hear what I said?"

Karan stopped, turned around and said with a hardened face, "I have many other important things to do. Tell Parul to go along with her and get the shopping done. She anyway has a better idea of ladies' stuff and its shops." Without waiting for any further reaction, he went inside the washroom and closed the door, but he could hear Kavya say, "Mummy, it's okay. I don't need to buy anything. I already have many suits at my home. I will tell Sundar bhaiya to bring them. My brothers are anyway coming tomorrow to see me off. Also, I have some new suits as well that I received at my wedding." Kavya had come out of the kitchen to lay the breakfast.

"But I wanted you to buy more and the stylish ones. You are moving now from a small town to a metropolitan city. Girls there dress so well. And you are so beautiful, educated, well-mannered and now the wife of a well-ranked government official. So, live like a memsahib, no lesser than the girls there." While Sarita said this with all the appreciation in her eyes for her daughter-in-law, Karan's father came in after his morning walk and just couldn't help but smile hearing his wife's suggestions for Kavya.

Parul too looked amused as she understood what her mother intended. All she wanted was to bring Karan closer to Kavya. Well behaved and good-natured Kavya in such a short span had won everybody's heart. There was no point anybody could ignore her or hate her. The only person who was reluctant to even look at her was Karan. Everyone was trying their bits to make life blissful for the newlyweds.

"Bhabhi, I will go with you. And I too need to buy a few things as well. And there's a big shop for bangles. They have the newest collection. And by now, I have known how fond you are of bangles. I have seen your collection. You can add a few more to it." Parul said coming close to her.

Kavya couldn't say no. She hadn't expected she would get so much love and support from her new family, especially after all that drama. God had been gracious to her.

Luggage was loaded into the taxi while Karan was having a chat with the driver standing beside the car. Jeevan along with Sarita stood there glad and all smiles to see their son and daughter-in-law leaving together for the big city to settle down in their married life.

"Time is a big healer and moreover with a better half like Kavya, Karan will soon be all settled in his domestic life," Jeevan said with a satisfactory smile.

Sarita nodded with moist eyes. She once again felt the guilt of the wrong decisions she had taken which had so deeply impacted her son's life snatching away all his happiness. But seeing Kavya, she felt strongly she would make a better wife than Jia or maybe she was getting biased as she never wanted at least a Punjabi bride for her son. She brushed away the thoughts that were trying to grip her mind. Whatever happened, happened for good and things are certainly going to be better- she convinced herself.

"You look so pretty dear. I am sure once you go there; everybody's eyes are going to be stuck on you. My brother is going to get a lot of compliments." Parul said lovingly looking at Kavya who was dressed in a heavily embroidered pastel suit with matching bangles adorning her slender hands and a red bindi highlighting her pretty face.

Sundar, Kundan, and Raja – Kavya's all three brothers had come to see their sister off. Turning towards Karan, Sundar said a bit loud but with a smile, "Jiju, wish you a happy journey and a happy life with my sister and need not remind you again, we are giving away our precious gem, Kavya to you. Never make her cry even by mistake."

Sunder kept gazing at Karan to read his facial reaction. Hardly he could notice anything on his expressionless face when Sarita came towards them saying, "Don't worry, all our blessings are with them. Everything is fine."

Kavya touched the feet of Karan's parents to receive blessings in abundance. Karan and Kavya sat inside the taxi and it left for Patna airport.

CHAPTER 7

The flight landed at New Delhi airport in the evening and Karan and Kavya came out with their luggage. All during the journey, Karan had hardly spoken anything to her. It was the first time Kavya had done the journey on a flight. She was ignorant of the proceedings at the airport, but she had just followed Karan, doing exactly what all he did. Only when Karan talked to her was when she was not able to tie her seat belt on the flight. He had ignored despite seeing her struggle with the belt but then later assisted her. And all while he did that, his eyes remained fixed on the belt. Kavya responded this gesture with a smile but he perhaps didn't notice as he looked away immediately after.

They got into the prepaid taxi and soon were in front of the building in Sushant Lok, Gurgaon where Karan lived.

Kavya looked around. It appeared to be a nice society with ample greenery and beautiful flowers planted around. There was a fountain and nearby, kids were running around in the play area. This was all new to her. At her hometown, there were no apartments; people had their houses while in Delhi NCR they call these bungalows. Her own house was in a sprawling area, but she liked the society, everything around looked good and well maintained. Karan moved towards the reception to take the lift.

The guard at the reception saluted Karan and then surprisingly looked at Kavya. A broad smile played on his face as he noticed the prominently visible mangalsutra resting around Kavya's neck and the red sindoor in her parted hair. "Sir, you got married. You never told us that you were going for your wedding." The guard immediately turned to Kavya saying folded hands, "Namaste madam, and welcome to the society. Any help you need, you can always ring me here."

Kavya responded folding her hands.

"Sir, you go. I will send the luggage to your flat." The guard said.

It was a two BHK apartment with a study and a beautiful view of the poolside. Kavya looked around and could see the mess of trash scattered on the sofa and some of the chairs. One of the bedrooms had a pile of clothes on an armchair, perhaps the ones that needed to be cleaned. Karan stood quietly for a while and then said, "That's the washroom. There is one inside the bedroom too. The maid comes in the morning to clean the house. The cook too comes in the morning and evening. I have informed them. They will be coming from tomorrow morning. So, today I will order something to eat. You may adjust your luggage in the bedroom. I will take my things to that bedroom." So, Karan made it clear that they wouldn't be sharing the same bedroom just like he did at his home.

It didn't come as a surprise to Kavya. In the last ten days, she was habituated to all this. At heart, she had accepted it. All she knew was that Karan was her man and she was falling in love with him despite all the indifference he showed.

"Why to order? I will cook for both for us." Kavya suggested.

"You must be tired. Don't take so much pain. And moreover, I don't think so there would be enough grocery in the kitchen. I will go and buy groceries and veggies after some time. But for today I will order. I prefer taking plain chapatis and vegetable and dal for dinner. Is that okay with you too or you want something else?"

Kavya was delighted to see him concerned about her. She knew he was a true gentleman and he would be concerned about anybody else he knew. Since her marriage, it was the first time that he had talked so much to her. It was to happen; just two people going to live under one roof couldn't remain isolated poles apart.

"I request you to let me check in the kitchen. I am not at all tired. I prefer taking food cooked at home especially after a journey. Nothing can match the taste of home-cooked food even if it is dal fry and roti. I know you too like it. Please allow me." Kavya said looking for his approval.

"Okay," Karan said and walked into the bedroom dragging the trolley. She had watched him closely in the last few days and had known likes and dislikes.

Kavya went into the kitchen and looked up different containers. There were enough flour and pulses. She checked the box of spices and there were some. Kavya went to the bedroom and quickly unzipped her luggage. She took out a suit to wear and rushed towards the washroom. She freshened up and then was back to the kitchen.

"Close the door. I will be back in some time," Karan said. He was dressed in a pair of pants that he wore at home.

In the next half an hour, Kavya was done with her work in the kitchen. Just then the doorbell rang. It was Karan having carry bags full of groceries and veggies in both the hands. He moved towards the kitchen when Kavya said, "Give me, I will keep them."

Karan didn't say a word and gave her the bags. As he walked

towards his room, Kavya said again stopping him, "Dinner is ready."

"Okay," came a short reply from him.

Kavya moved to the kitchen. She explored the polybags and found cucumber, beetroot, and tomato. She knew how fond of salads Karan was. His mother used to serve him with all the meals. Kavya quickly cut those veggies, squeezed half a lemon over it and sprinkled salt. And then she brought casserole containing chapati and other bowls on the table. She arranged plates on the table for both of them and stood to wait for him.

Karan came out and for a moment paused seeing her wait for him at the dining table. He said calm and grave, "Please don't stand like this and keep waiting for me. You can have your dinner whenever you want. I would be late coming back home most of the days and many times, I have dinner outside. This is not my parents' home. Here, you are free to do whatever you want." Karan sat pulling a chair.

Kavya too sat down and removed the lid of the casserole to serve chapati. Karan stopped her again, "I will do it myself."

Kavya pulled her hands back. She remembered he had stopped her earlier as well from serving her food. He did that himself.

"Since there was no vegetable in the house, I just cooked dal fry and chapatis. I have roasted papad and prepared some salad." Kavya said a bit scared what next he would say on that.

"I had already told you not to do all this. I would have ordered," Karan said. After a pause said further, "I prefer simple food" and concentrated on his plate.

Kavya saw him eating for a while and was satisfied seeing him eating peacefully. He was hungry no doubt as there had been a gap of several hours since they had something. Kavya had been cooking for several years now, all for her love of cooking but today she felt her culinary skills had been truly rewarded even though there wasn't a single word of praise to it.

It was ten at night and Kavya had unpacked her luggage and arranged properly. She came to the kitchen to take a bottle of water when she saw the door of the balcony open. And then through the slit, she could see her husband pacing while talking on his mobile. She knew who it was. For a while, she had forgotten there was somebody named Jia who ruled her husband's heart. Kavya quietly moved towards her room. She had accepted her fate!

It was seven in the morning when Kavya heard the call bell. She adjusted her nightgown and got out of her bed to open the door. Karan was still asleep. Kavya opened the door and seeing the lady at the door, Kavya could guess that she could be the maid or the cook. The lady looked at her awestruck and then greeted with a smile, "Namaste madam. I am a cook. Bhaiya never told him he was going to marry. The guard said he is married now."

"Yeah, it was sudden!" Kavya replied closing the door as the lady moved towards the kitchen.

Kavya followed the cook. The lady had taken out brinjals from the fridge. Kavya had expected the lady to ask her what had to be cooked but perhaps Karan had given her all the freedom to cook whatever she wanted. Kavya didn't say anything and just took a glass of water from the purifier.

The cook said while chopping the brinjals, "Bhaiya's marriage is a surprise to me. Did you two know each other beforehand?"

"No." Kavya replied in short.

"That's what!"

"What do you mean?" Kavya asked her with a raised eyebrow.

"Nothing," she said a bit hesitatingly.

Kavya kept gazing at her thinking perhaps she knew Jia and like everybody else it must be a surprise for her too. Kavya moved to the washroom to freshen up. And after some time, the call bell rang again and by then Karan had already got up. It was their maid.

Kavya came out of the washroom after taking a bath when she saw Karan sweating out on the treadmill. The maid who had come a few minutes back was busy cleaning the floor. Kavya went inside her bedroom and wiped her hair with the towel. She put a small bindi on her forehead and took out her box of bangles. She picked up a pair of the yellow bangles as they matched her suit. Suddenly she remembered Parul who would always admire her for her beautiful collection of bangles. Thought of Parul simply brought a dash of a smile on her face.

The cook was done with her work. She served the breakfast on the table and covered it with a plate. She didn't ask Kavya a word; she did it all the way she had been doing for some years now.

Karan was ready for his office. Dressed in black trousers and a light blue shirt, Karan looked a perfect gentleman, handsome and well-groomed. Kavya kept looking at her husband, his charm was hypnotic. Such was his aura that she had fallen in love with him, the very first time she had looked at his photograph her mother had given her saying it was her prospective groom. Karan took to the dining table for breakfast. Kavya poured water into the glass and sat beside him. She was still not able to take her eyes off her husband. She watched him lovingly as he slowly had his breakfast.

After finishing his breakfast, Karan took his laptop bag and moved towards the door as Kavya followed him.

"I will be late coming back since there is a lot of backlog," Karan said in his usual grave voice and moved towards the lift.

CHAPTER 8

"I will leave at six-thirty and will reach your place before seven." Karan talked on phone and concentrated back to a bunch of papers neatly placed in a file. Though he had been trying his best since morning to think about and do just his pending work, the news of his unexpected marriage had spread like fire in the entire office. His boss already knew the whole incident since Karan had informed him while at home. Karan was fed up answering to everyone – how, what, when and a lot of other things. He wasn't the one who could fabricate the truth and hence didn't try to hide how it all happened. But he simply hated remembering what had happened to him and how his life had changed in just a few days. Some congratulated him on his marriage, some sympathised with him the way it happened while some others still couldn't believe if it could happen this way! Karan just wanted to fly away somewhere, away from the crowd who were less concerned and more relished the unexpected happening like a spicy web series.

Karan looked at his watch; it was six thirty-five. He moved fast towards the parking. Though Jia's place wasn't far away, traffic in Gurgaon after the office hour could be horrible.

Jia's apartment was on the second floor and Karan always preferred taking the stairs. The door opened immediately he rang the bell. He knew Jia had been waiting impatiently and so was he, dying to meet her.

"Karan." Jia almost jumped and hugged him tightly.

Karan wrapped his arm around her waist pulling her close and not leaving an inch between them. They remained entwined, lost into each other's arms before Jia realised that the door was still open and somebody, perhaps the neighbour had just passed. Jia quickly closed the door and holding Karan's hand took him to the couch.

"Karan, I am still not able to come out of that shocking incident. How…" Jia said sitting close to Karan and looking deep into his eyes.

Karan could feel the pain in her voice. He had told her the sordid incident the very day he came back home after marriage. But still he knew how tough it was for both to believe that things had so much changed, their dream to get married had been challenged and terrifically slapped by fate but what remained was their love. Coming back to Jia was a relief and made him feel as if he had got his life back.

Karan looked at her holding her face in his palms and with loads of pain in his eyes, said in a choked voice, "I love you so much Jia and I can't even imagine a life without you. Why did this happen to me? Why? Everything has changed."

Jia took a deep sigh and said, "Not you and me dear. Our love remains the same." She brought her lips close to him and within seconds those two pairs of lips touched each other gently, caressed and were locked fiercely soon after. Truly nothing had changed between them. They had longed for each other during these days irrespective of whatever had happened in Karan's life. The fire was very much there within both! Her eyes seemed to be some intoxicating wine which was difficult for Karan to resist. It wasn't new for them. Their chemistry was solid, intact and unchanged. They knew they couldn't resist each other, perhaps not in any circumstance.

Karan lifted her in her arms and carried her to the bedroom, both not able to keep their eyes off each other. He made her lie down on the bed. They gazed at each other with a smile while Karan removed his shoes and came on top of her. He kissed her all over her face, his mouth willing to devour her. His lips came down kissing her neck and deep down her cleavage; his tongue trying to explore the skin beneath her satin dress. He pulled the string of her dress slowly taking it off and dumping it below the bed. Their bare skin crushed against each other till they moaned in the pleasure they had so much longed for in the last few days.

Jia lied comfortably in Karan's arms, her leg crossing his. "Karan, what about my name tattooed on your wrist?" She asked thoughtfully.

"That will remain as it is. You are my love and always be. No one can erase you out of my life," Karan said grave and confident.

"But you are married now to somebody else. What are we going to do now?"

"Jia, this is a marriage which has been forced on me without any fault of mine. My parents did something and those people reacted to it. And in this whole sordid drama, I am the only sufferer. But I am very clear that I can never accept that girl as my wife. Right now, everything looks dark and I really can't see anything beyond that." Karan said disappointed.

They remained quiet for moments and then Jia said, "Should I make us some coffee?"

"That would be good."

Jia got up and put on her dress lying on the floor. While Jia moved to the kitchen to make coffee, Karan too got back into his clothes and came out in the living.

They quietly sipped their coffee sitting on the couch near the glass window. Breaking the silence, Jia said, "I had heard about such marriages but never knew anything such happened in reality."

"Google it and you would find a lot of people falling victims to such groom kidnappings in Bihar. The reason is mostly dowry. But I never thought in rarest of my dreams that I too could be a victim to it."

"I am surprised by how your parents could do all that just for the sake of money?"

"It's all their greed for money which has made my life a mess. Though my mother has realised her fault, that's not going to change my life and to top it, she thinks Kavya is the perfect one for me and now I should settle down with her." Karan said, frustrated and angry.

"What nonsense? Are you some cattle that whenever needed you can be sold out to anyone or forcefully tied somewhere?"

"That's what they have been thinking of me."

"Karan, come out of this marriage. Report it to the police. This is so absurd!"

"Jia, it's not that simple. They are goons and they have strong links with politicians. More than that, they are insane. They are not one or two but an entire clan who would do anything against law. The problem is that I am not alone, I have my family there."

"So, what about us Karan?" Jia looked perplexed.

"I told you that girl means nothing to me. You are the first and the last girl in my life. I think with time, God will surely help me out of this trouble." Karan said thoughtfully.

Jia kept looking at Karan for a moment whose face suddenly turned pale talking about his marriage and without doubt, he was broken within. But she felt relaxed that at least her presence could make him feel better and bring a smile on his face.

"Let's order something for dinner. Though it's just a few days you were away but it seems like ages since we had our dinner together." Jia came to Karan and sat on his lap. Coming close to his ear, she whispered, "Love you so much".

"Love you too baby," Karan pulled her close to his chest and the two were kissing each other all over again.

After having their dinner, Karan and Jia stood in the terrace under the bright sky full of twinkling stars. They enjoyed the cold breeze as they talked about their work, friends and a host of other things.

Karan's phone lying on the table rang loud. Karan came to the pick up the phone and for a moment stopped seeing the name flashing on the mobile - it was Kavya. Karan glanced at the wall clock. It was 10 pm.

"Karan, who's calling?" Jia asked seeing him stand in a fix and staring at his phone.

He picked up the phone.

"When will you come home?" Kavya asked in a meek and subtle voice, a bit hesitant as well.

"I will come soon," Karan replied short and straight. And there was no further query from the other side.

"Was it Kavya?" Jia asked.

"Yes!"

"So, now she has started keeping a tab on you just like a concerned wife and you were answering her like a dutiful husband." Jia wasn't amused at all.

"She knows well where she stands in my life. She knows what the name Jia means to me. Had she been in my home town with my parents she would not have called. She is new to the city and all alone."

Jia could understand Karan's situation and the way he was disturbed, but any other guy would lose his mind. At least Karan was hopeful that with time, he could come out with some solution to his messed-up life.

It was ten-thirty at night. Kavya rushed to open the door as the bell rang.

Kavya welcomed in Karan with a pleasant smile. Without saying a word, Karan moved towards his room and kept his bag. Kavya followed him but only till the dining room and kept standing there looking at him. Karan closed the door to change and then came out. He moved towards the kitchen to get a glass of water, but he could see Kavya waiting for him at the dining table. He realised she could be waiting for him for dinner. That's what she did back at his parents' place if ever he was late for dinner. Though once irritated he had almost shouted at her not to do so but she remained quiet and perhaps unaffected as well.

He came back taking the glass of water and stood there for a while.

"I forgot to tell you that I won't be having dinner. I had it in my office since it got late." Karan informed her and moved towards his room.

Kavya kept gazing at him with a heavy heart as Karan pushed the door of his room to shut it. Somehow at the back of her mind, she knew he would have met Jia today. He talked to her everyday religiously. Every time she happened to look at her name inked on his wrist, she realised how much he loved her. Now when he was back to Gurgaon could he have resisted meeting the love of his life!

Kavya pulled a chair and sat to have her dinner though she didn't feel like having anything. She put a chapati on her plate and a bit of vegetable. Lost in her thoughts, she knew that's how her life was going to be but then with every dawn, forgetting everything and she would like to do every small thing for her man. She loved that! She loved him! And that was irrespective of the bitter truth she was aware of.

Kavya put her plate in the sink and wiped the kitchen slab. Switching off the light, she closed the door of the kitchen and paced towards her bedroom. For a while, she looked inside Karan's room through the slit of the door that remained slightly open. The light was still on. He usually slept not before eleven and he was right now on call in an uplift mood and Kavya could easily guess why.

Standing on her terrace, Kavya loved those sunrays that gently kissed her cheeks and freshened her mind. Every day, after finishing her daily chores, she would come out and bask in the sun. Back at home during winters, she used to sit for hours on the rooftop and read some Hindi novels by her favourite writers. She loved reading so much that she had made a library of hundreds of books. That was the only thing apart from bangles that she would spend money generously on. How beautiful and carefree days those were - she thought to herself but soon was pulled back to her present. She looked at those high-rise concrete buildings all around. It was one month since she had been into this life. She was Mrs. Karan Rai now. Her maid, milkman, the watchman, neighbours, people in the society, all knew her now as Mrs. Rai. Her in-laws cared for her so much. Her mother-in-law would regularly call her on her mobile phone. She may forget to talk to son for days but not Kavya. Parul is such love; she reminded her brother couple of days back that he should give his wife money for daily use. She would have easily guessed that Karan wouldn't have bothered about it. That's true he had his own world where she had no place. But one thing what Kavya strongly believed is that Karan was a gentleman with a soft heart who never intended to put anybody into trouble; not even her.

Though Kavya's parents had put enough money in her account, Karan being ignorant of this did release that she could need money to buy her own things. Kavya didn't even know the places where she could do her shopping. She didn't know anybody in the city. Also, she had been buying groceries with her own money that she had brought from home. Her heart went all out for him when he had come to her and said softly, "You should have asked me for money. There is a shopping complex and a mall nearby. I will take you today in the evening." And it was the most beautiful day of her life when she went out with her husband in the evening. Though Karan remained as usual grave and quiet all along she did shopping; she was more than happy that he was with her. Karan gave her enough cash so that she didn't have any shortage of money. Kavya avoided telling him about the money her father had put in her account just to avoid any ego clashes.

Kavya looked down at the florist shop in the society. They had perhaps got fresh white lilies. She was fond of flowers and preferred keeping fresh flowers in the vase rather than decorative artificial ones. She got her wallet from the bedroom and moved downstairs locking the door behind.

Kavya paid the florist and took the bunch of white lilies. A lady standing nearby smiled and greeted her, "Hi, I am Smriti. I live in the same building on the 3rdfloor."

"Hi, I am Kavya." Kavya answered to the lady dressed in a cotton saree and holding a hand bag.

"You are Karan's wife, right? Karan knows me and my husband well. I saw you many a times buying groceries but somehow couldn't interact. Would you like to come to my home and have a cup of tea? Neighbours should always know each other!" The lady smiled saying the last few words.

"Yeah sure." Kavya replied instantly. She found the lady decent and moreover she wanted to know people around. In fact, she wanted to have some friends in the society to overcome her loneliness that was gripping her with every passing day.

They came to Smriti's flat and Smriti made Kavya comfortable offering her a glass of water. "I just came back from school. I am a Social Science teacher at Soham International. It was a parent-teacher meeting day and hence an early off for the school. My husband would be back at around six in the evening. Till then, I am all free. I will quickly get us cups of tea."

Kavya looked around and found a photograph hung on the wall. She could guess it would be Smriti and her husband happily smiling in the photo; it was their wedding photograph. Kavya kept watching it and somewhere at the back of her mind she could feel her heart ache for blissful married life. People may not have a perfect life but at least they have photos to call perfect. She didn't even have that. All her wedding photographs were not even worth cherishing.

Smriti was back with cups of tea. She offered Kavya and sat beside her.

"Are you new to the city Kavya or have visited Gurgaon before?" Smriti asked sipping the tea.

"Completely new. Marriage has brought me here." Kavya replied looking at an elegant looking Smriti and trying to judge her age. She would be around thirty, she guessed.

"Karan used to talk a lot whenever we met earlier but since he is back from home this time, he has been so quiet. Even my husband noticed this. Perhaps I shouldn't ask this but since I can see some pain in your eyes and a usually sad face which a newlywed bride doesn't have, I can't hold back myself. Are you two not happy with the marriage?" Smriti asked, her eyes fixed on Kavya.

Kavya wasn't prepared for this unexpected question. She looked away for a moment. She knew this query would be in everybody's mind who knew Karan but Smriti had asked her outrightly.

Seeing her mum, Smriti said, "I am really sorry if I hurt you asking this, but I just remembered my own days. I wasn't happy when I got married to my husband. I was in love with someone, but destiny never works according to your sweet will. I couldn't accept my husband for almost couple of years but then with time I realised he is the best thing that could happen to me. I wore the same grief in my eyes as you do but I find that with Karan too and both of you seem to be hit hard."

Smriti was right. Kavya had been tight-lipped and never spoke anything about her marriage or her life post marriage. She had suppressed all her pain deep inside but today she somehow felt like speaking out and releasing her deep buried emotions.

"Ours is a case of groom kidnapping. Karan was abducted to marry me. I don't know whether you have heard about it," Kavya's voice was painful.

"Oh my God, really? Yes, I have heard about some cases in Bihar."

"Yes, unfortunately we too are a victim to it. Rather I would say Karan has been a victim to it. There's a long story behind it but all I can say is both our parents are responsible for this whole mess that our lives have become. His parents' greed and my parents' ego to settle the score has landed us in this situation. I had so much opposed this forced wedding, but nobody listened to me. Though my in-laws have realised their fault and sooner or later perhaps my parents too would realise, but can it ever mend the damage? No." Kavya spoke her heart out.

Smriti was quiet for a moment and then said, "Don't you think that with time, everything would be fine and you two would be happy together as husband and wife?"

"I always try to maintain this false hope, but my heart repeatedly says it may not be possible."

"And why is it so? You are young, beautiful, and graceful and after meeting you, I can perceive you are good natured too. To run a marriage, all you need is a partner who can understand and respect you. And both of you, I feel, can complement each other."

"Karan is a nice man. I have always accepted this."

"And what I can understand is you like him. Right?"

Kavya smiled and said, "You seem to be good at reading mind and heart."

Smriti laughed out at the compliment. "You can say that."

"Things are not that simple as it may seem. Marriage may have been forced on him but love and emotions that he carries for somebody can't be forced to die. That will prevail. I can't replace her." Kavya said somewhat lost.

"You mean Jia?" Smriti asked.

Kavya was taken aback. "You know her?"

"Yes. I have met her. She used to come here at his apartment quite often. Karan had once introduced her as a good friend. Later he told us they were together. Yes, I found them very much in love. They looked fabulous together. But all said and done, I again say the same thing - destiny would not act according to your sweet will. If we can't do anything to it, we need to accept it and move on. That's it!" Smriti said looking straight into her eyes.

Kavya was silent, disappointed by this dismal game of destiny.

Smriti put her hand on Kavya's shoulder. "Keep loving, love will come back to you."

Kavya didn't know how true it would be. One truth that she couldn't deny was that she loved Karan and her love for him was getting stronger with every passing day. It's rightly said - love is selfless and it would prevail even if you don't get it in return. That's its beauty!

Kavya felt nice meeting Smriti. She had found somebody in this alien city with whom she could share her feelings and confide in as a friend.

Kavya had given off to the cook. It was Sunday and Karan wasn't in a hurry to leave for office. Kavya so much loved cooking a variety of dishes and somehow, she never had the satisfaction from the food prepared by her cook. Today she had made up her mind to talk to Karan to remove the cook and allow her to prepare the meals. However hard she had tried to explain the cook to put less oil and spices, she could never understand the right proportions. A day or two she would remember Kavya's instructions but then she would be back to square one. Kavya knew Karan always preferred less oil and spices but he would never complain. He anyways had only breakfast regularly at home, lunch was in office canteen and dinner hardly twice or thrice in a week. But he took care to inform her if he didn't have dinner at home. He would tell her that he would have dinner with colleagues or outside with friends. But Kavya had known by now that it was Jia with whom he had dinner most of the days in the week. He would spend time with her after the office hours and come back home at ten or eleven. She had heard him many a times calling her back after he reached home. Even on most of the weekends, he would spend time with Jia. Kavya would spend the whole day either watching TV, reading novels which she had got from a nearby book store or catching up with Smriti. Talking to Smriti always gave her emotions an outlet. Smriti would take her to parlour, shopping and nearby cafes to hang out. Kavya tried to keep herself busy but her heart did pain every time she realised her husband would be with Jia, but then she had accepted that she was the other woman in their life. And there was nothing she could do except for leaving everything to destiny. She wasn't sure of future, but she had to live her present. One thing that made her feel good is that even though Karan spent hours out of home be it in office or with Jia, he would come back home at the end of the day. Being a nice and kind-hearted man, he was, perhaps he cared for her not to let her be alone at night. Her love and respect for Karan had only multiplied.

Kavya peeped from inside the kitchen, Karan had got up. The tea was also ready. She placed the cup of tea on a tray and moved towards Karan's room, though she stood at door. She never went to Karan's room if he was inside and until told her to come in.

Karan saw her through the sides of the newspaper that he had held in his hand. "Please come." He said keeping the paper aside.

"Tea!" Kavya said putting the tray on the bed.

"Thanks so much." Karan said and this time a smile of gratitude visible on his face. Karan never asked for tea from Kavya but she would as a routine offer him in the morning and evening if at all he was back to home on time. Earlier he used to blatantly and rudely tell her not to do anything for him. She would be visibly disappointed but that never affected her. She kept doing every small thing she could for him. She arranged his room, cleaned his cupboard and made his bed when he left for office.

At one point of time, Karan was irritated to an extreme. It even brought Kavya to tears. She said, "I am all alone in the house for the whole day. Please let me do these. At least this would keep me busy." Drops of tears had trickled down her eyes. Karan did realise later that she indeed was too alone. He had Jia, but she had no one.

Spending those few days at her in-laws' place Kavya had known all his likes and dislikes. Aloo puri was his favourite, he never ate pumpkin, any strand of hair if found in the kitchen or food turned him off, jalebi rabri was his favourite dessert, actions movies he would die for, blue his favourite colour when it came to clothing and many more things which Kavya knew and Karan did notice this.

Karan glanced at Kavya who was still standing quietly.

"Do you want to say something?" He asked.

"Yeah," Kavya said a bit hesitatingly. "We are paying so much to our cook and I don't see that worth. I know she has been here for some years now but still I would request you to allow me to cook. I had always loved cooking at my home. Please allow me…"

Kavya almost begged for that and Karan could watch her face that hoped for a positive response from him.

Karan nodded. "Okay, pay her for the whole month and let her go."

Karan's affirmative reply brought an instant smile on her face. But she still stood there.

"Still something?" Karan asked.

"Could you please buy a baking oven?" She hesitated, asking for something.

"Okay I will give you my card. There is a good electronic store nearby. If possible, take Smriti along with you and get it from the store." Karan took out his credit card from his wallet and gave it to Kavya. "Password is my year of birth…"

"I know!" Kavya said before he could finish. "I mean your year of birth. Thanks so much!"

Karan hadn't seen her in such fine and bright mood ever before. They hadn't even talked this long ever before!

CHAPTER 9

The mobile that was on silent mode had been flashing for quite some time. Karan picked up the call as he got free from the conference.

"So busy? Where were you?" It was Sumoy on the other side.

"Sorry dear. I just got free from a conference."

"Maya told me to remind you again. You two have to reach the party venue by seven in the evening."

"Sumoy, I will come but please don't tell me to bring Kavya along. Maya and you have known all; nothing is hidden from you. This marriage hasn't changed anything between me and Jia. We are very much together as we were. You know that! And I would not offend Jia taking Kavya along with me to the party." Karan made it clear.

Maya took over the phone from Sumoy; perhaps it was on speaker. "Karan, both you and Jia have been our friends right from our college days and we love you both. Jia is a darling to me but Karan you can't ignore the fact that you are married for over six months now, living with a girl who is your wife under the same the roof in the same house. Whatever be your equations, people know you two as husband and wife. For the world, Kavya is not the other woman but Jia is. This is the fact!" Maya spoke out all in a stretch. She paused a bit and continued gently, "Karan, as a woman, I can understand well the feelings of a woman specially a wife who is neglected, unwanted, undesired and no one to fall back on in this city. To top it all, she doesn't even complain of anything. You would be called to many parties and occasions and people would expect you to come with your wife. Till this married tag is with you, you can't ignore this. Moreover, I really want to meet Kavya. Jia is out of town for her official trip. So, anyway they won't confront each other. Karan, please it's a request."

Maya's power-packed words had almost silenced Karan and he didn't want to offend his closest friends. "Okay, we would come." Karan said after a while.

"That's good. See you then in the evening."

Karan called up Kavya and informed her to be ready in the evening for the party.

"Smriti, seriously, I don't know what to wear. How to get ready? I am so nervous." Kavya said a bit worried.

"First of all, I am so happy for you that Karan wants you to come along with him to his friends' party. After so many months of marriage, finally there are some changes in him! See, that's the power of being a wife. Whatever be the relation between a husband and a wife, people would look at you as a couple." Smriti said feeling good for Kavya.

Kavya took a deep sigh. "It's nothing like that dear. Yes, he does care for me, listens to me. But there is no consummation. It is an unconsummated relationship. And taking me along with him is just a social obligation." Kavya's voice became a bit low while uttering those last few words.

Smriti put her hand on a dejected Kavya and said, "Come on dear, now cheer up. Don't think much and leave all your worries behind. Now let's go for your shopping and then you need to visit the parlour as well.

Kavya stood before her dressing mirror looking at her matte finished, luscious lips. A feeling of satisfaction surfaced in her eyes seeing her tall curvaceous body in the well-fitted black gown. She had left her hair loose in light curls. It was the first time she had donned up something like this. Her mirror image said she looked stunning and she did realise that. Back at home, her beauty had attracted many and she had a long list of suitors though she never was interested in any of them. The only one man she ever got interested in was Karan. And today she was waiting for him, her husband, to accompany him for the party. She did feel a bit nervous thinking of Karan's reaction on seeing her in altogether different get up. She was unsure whether she was able to match up to his standards. Lot of things kept floating in her mind when she heard the bell ring.

She opened the door and as expected it was Karan. Karan stepped in and for a moment his eyes were locked into her, though he soon realised that awkward situation which could leave a false impression of him being captivated by her charm. He moved ahead towards his room without a reaction, but he did notice that Kavya certainly looked stunning in the transformed look. He had always seen her in a suit or a saree and a look that was typical of a small-town girl. But he too accepted in heart this girl was really something and had the guts to handle any situation with ease. And among all these she had never complained of anything. Karan noticed Kavya was still standing there. He turned around and said, "Give me ten minutes. I will just get ready."

Kavya knew there won't come a reaction from Karan as to how she looked. Though while coming from parlour from the main gate of her society to her apartment, she had noticed admiration in many eyes. Smriti had already complemented her - "You are born with the grace that no one can beat."

Kavya waited for Karan. After some time, he came out dressed in a black suit looking absolutely dashing. Kavya knew her husband with his well-built, sharp features, a charming face and a dimpled smile was a head turner. She wasn't sure if at all and to what extent she could match up to him today.

"Okay, let's go!" Karan said looking at her for a second and moved towards the door.

Kavya took her clutch bag and a bit hesitantly asked him, "Am I looking fine?" Karan turned around to glance at her all over again when Kavya further said, still hesitatingly, "I mean…my dress…I mean, hope it is not odd?"

Karan could well understand the worries gripping her mind. Putting her to ease, he replied, "All good."

It was a short and simple reply but good enough to put to rest all her doubts regarding her appearance.

All through the drive, they kept quiet, those two words - "all good" kept tossing in Kavya's mind and that gentle but killer smile on Karan's face - it had made her heart race. He was nice to her, cared for her needs and off late took her as a responsibility though there was nothing beyond. She stood nowhere in his life. But she always tried to find that little bit of happiness in whatever Karan did for her even though her heart couldn't ignore the fact that she was a burden on him; a forced responsibility.

"Hey Karan, come. We were waiting for you," Maya said, greeting him as Sumoy too joined.

"Congratulations both of you on the success of your start up. I am proud of you guys. I sincerely wish your venture keeps touching new heights." Karan said almost forgetting Kavya who stood behind him.

Kavya stood quietly as Maya happened to glance at her. "You are Kavya!"

Kavya smiled looking at her while Karan realised that he should at least for courtesy introduce Kavya to his friends.

"Kavya, this is Sumoy and Maya, his wife. We are friends since our college days." Karan was crisp and short in introduction.

"Hey Kavya, so nice to meet you. Please come." Sumoy led them to other guests.

"Karan, she is so pretty. I had never imagined you had married such a sweet girl." Maya whispered into Karan's ear as a bit demure looking Kavya stood beside her husband.

"Kavya, come with me I will introduce you to our other guests. We mostly have our common friends who know Karan and you would love to meet our gang." Maya took Kavya along with her.

Karan didn't seem amused at all. All the parties he had attended till now were with Jia and his entire friend circle knew they were inseparable. He and Jia were always the toast of the parties or any get together. And today she wasn't with him and he so much missed her. His face turned dull and mood not the usual self. He could watch the mixed reactions on people's faces when Maya introduced Kavya to them as his wife. Kavya instead of Jia was a surprise for most of them.

"Karan, come on dear. Don't keep yourself aloof. I can understand what you would be going through. But friend, forget everything as of now and enjoy the party." Sumoy put his arm around his shoulder and tried to cheer up his friend.

Karan noticed Kavya had soon mingled with guests and the slight hesitation that she carried while she came here, was gone. Though she spoke in Hindi, she looked graceful and well groomed.

Kavya was busy talking to a lady who seemed quite interested in discussing a piece that Kavya had written for a Hindi magazine. Maya came to Karan and looking at Kavya for a while said admiringly, "Karan, I must admit Kavya is such a sweet and talented girl. She has such deep hold on almost everything happening around in the country; be it economy, foreign diplomacy or any damn thing. She has an opinion of her own. And she occasionally writes for journals as well. I am impressed man."

Karan listened quietly. Even he didn't know so much about her; he had never bothered to find out.

"You know Karan when you had told about this unexpected marriage of yours, I got the image of a girl who would be rustic, not so educated, may be arrogant because of the family she comes from; I mean all negative things about her came to my mind. But she is so different rather I would say a woman of substance!" Maya said in a flow but soon realised Karan was indifferent to it. Perhaps that had to be as it was Jia and not Kavya who ruled his mind and heart.

"You have wonderful guests. The lady I was talking to is a journalist with a Hindi daily," Kavya said as she joined Karan and

Maya.

"Yeah, she is our friend and a regular at page three parties. She seemed impressed with you. Would you like to have a drink?" Maya asked a bit sceptical if Kavya ever had alcohol as the waiter stood with glasses of hard drinks.

"I never had alcohol earlier." Kavya replied.

"There is always a first time if you wish." Maya winked.

Kavya looked at Karan who remained indifferent and expressionless holding his drink.

"Okay," Kavya replied gently. She knew it would hardly matter to her husband if she had a drink or not.

Maya handed her a glass of beer.

Kavya realised she should have taken a little less beer although she was balanced but not her usual self. While on the way back home, she had tried talking to Karan couple of times, to which he had replied only in monosyllables. Now, back home, she kept her clutch bag on the table and turned to Karan coming almost close to him. "Thanks for taking me along with you. It was an evening well spent. In fact, after a long time, I felt so happy." She kept gazing into his eyes, her love for him vividly visible. Karan remained unaffected and yet again devoid of expression.

Kavya turned towards her room saying good night to him. She stopped and walked back to Karan.

"You look handsome," she said with her glare transfixed on him. "You are a nice person." She said and then she walked towards her room.

Karan had never seen this facet of her. She had always been shy, quiet and hesitant in front of him. It was the alcohol-effect, Karan guessed. But today in the party, Kavya was a different girl altogether - smart, graceful, bold and certainly nowhere that shy and quiet person. The way she carried herself no one could say, she was from a small town of Bihar and that too from a family of goons. A perfect misfit! Karan could feel this marriage was difficult for her as well. Moreover, she knew he met Jia almost every day. She knew the reason he came late at night and with whom he had been spending time or for that matter why he usually didn't have dinner at home. Kavya had seen the messages from Jia popping up on his cell phone screen whenever it lay on the table; those kisses, those love messages. Many a times, she brought the mobile to him when there was a call from "Honey" and certainly she wasn't that ignorant to not understand who this "Honey" was. And of course, his tattoo on his wrist was enough to remind her of a woman who was his love interest. At times Karan failed to understand why this girl never complained. Certainly, she would have the pain of not having the bliss of a satisfying married life, but she never let it show on her face. Even in the party, she behaved as if everything was so normal! Karan felt pity for her but then his life wasn't good as well!

CHAPTER 10

"I had missed you so much these days. Please don't take such long trips. I had almost died for you," Karan whispered. Jia was in his arms and the two were sprawled on the couch.

"You know dear, even I don't want to go away from you. It was really urgent, couldn't be avoided." Jia kissed him on his bare chest which she had already unbuttoned.

"Jia, now it's difficult without you. I have been fighting every single day within myself. I feel someday, I would go mad and my family may have to take me to a mental asylum."

"Please don't say this. And have you ever thought about me; what my heart goes through seeing you live with some other woman. We were together for years, we dreamt of a beautiful life together and then suddenly another woman came into your life. People regard her as your better half and I stand nowhere." Jia said hurt and irritated.

"You know dear, this marriage has absolutely no meaning for me."

"Then why are you carrying this burden? Why don't you come out of it?" Jia threw a question that put Karan to thoughts making him realise he needed to come out of this whole mess as soon as possible. Seeing him thoughtful, Jia continued, "Karan till when is it going to continue like this? We need to decide if we really have a future together. My family wants me to get settled and I really can't push off my marriage for a long time. I love you, but you need to understand dear that I am the only kid of my parents and can obviously not hurt them. They know under what circumstances you have been married and just for my sake they are all willing to wait till you come out of all this but then you need to take a decision." Jia was calm but amply clear.

Still quiet and pondering a bit, Karan said, "Yes, I do need to take a decision as this is not how I am going to spend and spoil my whole life. I know what I have to do."

"What?" Jia asked eagerly.

"Parul has finished her graduation and we are looking for a suitable match for her. Hopefully things are going to be fixed soon. Once she is married, I will file for divorce and I seriously now give a damn to those goons. Let them do whatever they want, I am going to fight them in any case. Getting scared and not taking any step is only going to bolster the morale of all those who have made marriage a joke by groom kidnapping. If Kavya's family think they married off their girl putting me at a gunpoint and given her a happy life, I will show them what reality can be. There can never ever be any relation between me and that girl. Marriages are supposed to be made in heaven, but they have gifted her virtual hell and this can end only when this marriage ends. Let those fuckers do whatever they want. I will see them!"

"That's my Karan, bold and daring. My family and I are always there to support you in any way possible. And believe me; they can't me mightier than law," Jia said encircling her arms around his neck and gently rubbing her lips against his.

Karan got up from the couch and holding her hand took her to the bed.

"I am not going home today," he said looking at his ladylove.

"Seriously? And what about her?"

"I am going to call her and let her know that I would be staying back at some colleague's place."

"Superb. After a long time, we are spending a night together." A naughty smile played on Jia's face.

Karan called up Kavya and informed her. She didn't object or question anything; just replied with an "okay" but sounded low and depressed. Karan kept his phone aside on the table but for a moment he couldn't avoid thinking about Kavya. It was surprising she didn't say anything, but she sounded low. She certainly understood he would be with Jia all night. Karan tried to push her away from his thoughts but couldn't. What kind of a girl she is! She never complains about anything to anybody, has never revealed the real scenario of their married life to her family, never put up any demand from him, never got possessive of him or never even questioned about Jia despite knowing their relation. Karan really failed to understand her.

"What happened? What did she say?" Jia asked trying to read this face.

"Nothing."

"Really? Surprising! She doesn't have any objection. Sometimes, I doubt if she has some affair or what. A small-town girl comes to a metro with her husband, doesn't have a conjugal life or anything of a man and wife and is still living happily without any concerns or complaints. How is it possible?" Jia said thoughtfully.

Karan came closer to Jia and muttered "I don't think so. I feel she is in love with me. What I could get she had willingly agreed to the marriage proposal when my parents had visited her. She had just seen my photo and had given a nod! But then her hopes just went downhill."

"I seriously, can't believe all this. Everything that's happened or still is happening sounds bizarre. And this girl is a mystery to me," said Jia.

"All I can understand, she has deep feelings for me and perhaps she just wants me to be happy. That's why she hasn't ever complained of anything." Karan said curtly. After a short silence, he said looking at her passionately, "Let's forget everything. Right now, it's you and I; our love would conquer all hurdles. Nothing could be mightier than our love. We would be together forever." Karan pulled her and allowed her to lie down with him. Pressing her beneath, he kissed her neck and then passionately started caressing all over her face.

"Karan…" Jia murmured.

"Yeah baby, am I hurting you?"

"No. I feel you have a soft corner for Kavya."

"What? Is this what going on in your mind?" Karan stared at her aghast.

"I felt so."

"I am just being kind to her till the time she is with me. That girl is harmless to me, to us. You can see that. My life has certainly been a mess because of her family but she is in a worse condition. I can understand she has suppressed her grief inside and has been smiling. I have you, but she has no one. I really can't imagine how I would have pulled on had I been in her place with no one to fall back on. But don't tell me that she is making you feel insecure in anyway.

Though I am amused to see that you are so possessive about me and I love that baby."

"The thing that constantly bugs me is that she is your wife and that's how the world would recognise her."

"She is no one for me. And let the fucking world go to hell! I have told you at the right time I would divorce her." Karan said in a stretch, the mood that was set to romance was almost lost. He lied down beside Jia, quiet.

"Hey sweetheart, I am sorry to spoil your mood. I really didn't mean to do that. I love you to the moon and back. Now please smile." Jia came on top of him, bent a bit and thrust her mouth on his, making him part his lips as their tongues explored each other. Jia tossed and pulled Karan on top of her. Her lips caressed his naked neck and soon they started making passionate love which kept them awake well into the night.

Kavya stood before the tall mirror and picked up the small silver box lying on the dressing table. She took a pinch of red sindoor out of it and neatly put into the mid partition of her somewhat wet hair that was let loose at the back. It wasn't a trend here to use thick strand of powdered sindoor, and women usually used a small dot or just a thin red line, but Kavya loved her roots and growing up seeing her mother use it that way, she had always secretly wished to do it exactly like that. Then she picked up some more of the powder and with her finger made a dot like bindi on her forehead.

"Bhabhi, you are looking so pretty. Perfect Indian lady!" The maid who was cleaning the floor, stopped for a while and said with an admiration for her in her eyes.

Kavya looked at her own image for a while; in a pink and white floral suit, bangles, mangalsura, bindi and the red sindoor adorning her hair, she did look an ideal Indian married woman. This is the image Kavya always had in her mind during her growing years. Kavya never had any high ambitions; she just wanted to be a wife who would love, care and be solely dedicated to her hubby, and his home which she would nurture with every bit of her affection. She was trying to do everything that she could out of her capacity, suppressing the heartache and ignoring the harsh reality of her life where marital bliss was a mirage.

"You know, you are an ideal wife that any Indian boy would love and feel privileged to have in his life. I hope your husband understands someday." The maid had sympathy for Kavya as she was aware of the equations between Karan and Kavya.

Kavya had always treated her maid well and the maid too respected her. She knew about Jia and Karan's relationship. At times during their random conversation, the maid had talked to Kavya about Jia. She had told her that many a times Jia would spend her night and even stay here for a couple of days. At times, when she came for work in the morning, Karan would open the door while Jia would be asleep the bedroom in her tiny night dress. Nothing was hidden to the maid; maids usually know more than the insiders know about a family.

Seeing the pains on Kavya's face the maid tried to make her hopeful, "Bhabhi, whatever be the past, marriage is one pious institution that everybody should respect. It's good that at least after your marriage, bhaiya has maintained a decency of not bringing her home anytime. I haven't seen her. Why doesn't he now remove that tattoo from his hand?"

Kavya had no words to reply to her maid. She herself didn't know which way her life was flowing and what was in store for her in future. She had already left everything to God. The maid was still sitting on the ground on her feet, looking at her and the floor cleaning cloth mop kept aside; perhaps she waited to hear something from her.

"Mithidi (that's how Kavya called her maid), there are certain things which are better to be left to time. The God is a gamer and knows who to be given what and when. Now, quickly you finish up the work and I would move go to the kitchen to make tea for Karan." While moving to the kitchen, Kavya just glanced inside Karan's room; he was taking out clothes from his wardrobe. Perhaps, willing to take a shower. He had come back home just a few minutes back at around ten in the morning after being away for the whole night. It was the weekend and he looked quite relaxed in doing his stuff.

Kavya quickly prepared the ginger tea in all milk, something which Karan preferred. Taking the tray, she paused at the door which was already open, knocked once and moved inside.

"Tea for you," she offered the cup to Karan with a smile that naturally played on her lips whenever she faced him.

"I had black coffee in the morning but no worries; I will have this as well." He kept the cup on the tool and sat down on his bed picking up The Economics Times which Kavya necessarily kept every morning on his bed.

Kavya turned to move out of the room when she happened to glance at the laptop bag which Karan had kept on the bed.

"Laptop bag looks dirty. Should I get it cleaned?" Kavya asked.

"Yeah, that would be great." Karan replied and then

immediately his cell phone started ringing.

Kavya unzipped the bag to empty it while she heard Karan talk on the phone in a low-pitched voice- "Yeah, just reached around twenty minutes back. Will a take a shower now."

Kavya could guess whom he was talking to. She had this in her mind that his night stay was nowhere else but at Jia's place. She held her emotions back letting it not surface. She kept the laptop on the bed. There was a notebook too which she took out, but it somehow slipped out of her hand and fell on the floor along with some visiting cards that were inside the notebook. She picked all those and opened the notebook to keep them back. And then, she saw the name written inside – Jia. It was Jia's notebook with some technical jargons written inside. So, Karan was certainly with Jia yesterday and perhaps by mistake her notebook was kept inside Karan's laptop bag. Kavya kept it on the laptop lying on the bed and peeked into the bag for anything else. And then she found a small packet in the front pocket. She stood still for a moment to see the packet of condom. She kept it below the notebook with a tormented heart and eyes about to burst out.

Karan had kept the phone and got engrossed into the newspaper while sipping his cup of tea. He didn't at all notice the stuffs Kavya kept on the bed and or when she quietly walked away with the laptop bag.

Kavya gave the bag to the maid to clean and moved towards her room. She shut the door and bumped into her bed as tears rolled down her cheek uncontrolled. Didn't she know the stark truth? She did. Karan and Jia were into a relationship for long and there was no way she could avoid the possibility of their intimate relationship. So, why now this emotional breakdown? She questioned her inner self. She had tried to ignore everything and move on. But truth is bitter and brutal. It couldn't be any way ignored as it would surface anytime blatantly as it did now! But how to control this stupid heart that desires things that are beyond reach. Kavya felt helpless.

Karan came out of the washroom wiping his hair with the towel when he noticed Jia's notebook kept on the laptop. He remembered he had taken Jia's notebook for something urgent and by mistake kept it inside his laptop bag. He picked up notebook thinking if Kavya would have turned the leaves and seen Jia's name? And then he glanced at the packet of condom lying on the laptop.

"Oh God! I forgot it was inside the bag. So, she kept it here." Karan thought to himself and felt somewhat embarrassed. He peeped out of his room looking for Kavya but she wasn't around. Despite everything being known to her, now even more clearly, Kavya didn't say a single word. Karan failed to understand if really somebody could be so compromising. He knew his future and he was determined that sooner or later he would put an end to this marriage. But why is this girl mum? She could speak out the truth to her family or his family or could even talk to him directly. If she is living in the false hopes of having a conjugal life with him any time in future, then certainly she would be left broken.

The maid called out Kavya seeing the door of her room closed from inside, "Bhabhi, I am leaving. Shut the door." She said and moved out hurriedly as she had another house to go to.

After a while, wiping the tears off and forcefully trying to make her face look normal without leaving any track of her emotional outburst, Kavya came out and shut the main door. She looked at the wall clock, it had struck eleven. She brought out the casserole containing stuffed cauliflower paratha and a bowl of mint raita. Being health conscious, Karan avoided having them frequently but usually on weekends, Kavya prepared parathas or aloo puri for breakfast. Kavya had picked up all these favourites of Karan from her initial stay with Karan's family. Karan too had never objected to whatever she prepared.

"Come and have breakfast," she said standing outside Karan's room, her voice low and a bit choked.

Karan came out and instantly his gaze moved out to Kavya's face. He had guessed it right. Kavya was certainly not in her normal mood. Her swollen and somewhat red eyes were vividly visible to Karan. He knew what had caused that. As usual she never spoke out anything but time to time her faded pale face would tell Karan everything. And today too after facing the reality which she already knew, she broke down. Karan many a times felt pity for Kavya. But there was hardly anything he could do. He just wanted to clear the chaos that his life was.

CHAPTER 11

Kavya came out in the living room and while rubbing her eyes looked at the wall clock. It was five thirty in the morning. She had got up a bit early today. After all, it was an important day for her…her first teej. She wanted to prepare the breakfast for Karan well before time and then start with the rituals. Kavya tied up her hair into a bun and moved into the kitchen. She had already prepared the batter for dosa as today she had planned some South Indian delicacies for Karan. In half an hour, she was done cooking dosa and coconut chutney and kept the food on the dining table. Kavya noticed Karan had got up and got the newspaper lying outside the door. Sitting on the bed, his back resting against the pillow, he was keenly going through the headlines. Kavya prepared the tea and took inside his room.

Karan quietly took the cup of tea while Kavya hurried towards the washroom to take a shower. Karan never wanted Kavya to do anything for him as this simply put him in an uncomfortable position. A pseudo and totally meaningless marriage that it was to him, taking advantage of all the comforts that Kavya was providing him in day to day life simply added to his guilt. But even though he didn't want these, things had moved on at its own pace. He just couldn't stop her from doing whatever she did for him. Kavya's innocence had stopped him saying anything harsh to her and moreover he knew it wasn't far away when he would legally separate from her. His mind had already taken a strong stand.

Kavya draped a maroon and green hued bandhani print saree with beautiful work all along the border. She had done all the shopping for teej a few days ago along with Smriti. She had asked Karan if he was free for shopping but somehow his schedule was too hectic and moreover, he was now used to saying her to go shopping with Smriti. He knew she had found a good friend in her.

Karan was ready in his office wear and came to the breakfast table. Kavya served him breakfast. Karan did notice that Kavya had specially dressed but he couldn't gather if there was something special today. With that big red bindi and thick and vividly visible strain of sindoor in her middle-parted hair, she reminded him of some deity with an aura around her. She did look stunning; a true image of an Indian beauty with all those cultures intact. A girl that any Indian boy would without a hitch accept happily as his partner for life- he was forced to think for a while but then he was not the man for her. Their paths were different, accidentally crossed but never to converge again. Karan put a rest to those bubbles of thoughts and got to his plate to finish up his breakfast. Just then, his mobile phone got ringing. The call was from his mother.

"Yeah ma, I am having my breakfast and would be leaving for office," Karan said.

"You should take leave today. Kavya is fasting today for teej." His mother reminded him of the festival.

Karan was silent for a moment. Now, he gathered why Kavya was dressed up in the new saree. And it was teej-shopping that she had asked him for but later she went with Smriti.

With Karan being mum, his mother on the other side continued, "Karan, this is a big festival for married women. She is fasting for you; you know she won't take even water. You should be with her throughout the day and take her to the temple. Usually there is a long queue in temples today. She is all alone there and would be doing all the rituals, making prasad; everything on her own. You need to be with her."

Karan was never amused to listen any preaching from his family members regarding his married life. He would just think- why can't these people understand that no amount of preaching or effort from them is a going to do any good to his marriage and make Kavya and him a happily married couple and thinking off erasing his love for Jia was not even a remote possibility. Who told her to fast for him? Why can't everybody just let him live? He felt frustrated, sick and utterly irritated but somehow controlled his angst and replied as calm as he could be, "Ma, I can't take leave. There is some urgent meeting today at office."

"Can't you manage for one day?

"No. And ma please don't pressurise me for things that are not possible." This time Karan was hard and clear.

Sarita preferred not saying anything further or it could spoil his mood and that was only going to affect Kavya. Things should go smooth on this auspicious day and that's what she wanted. "Okay, try to come on time in the evening. You usually are late back home. I never knew that even government jobs could be so hectic."

"I will see if I can. Now, I need to leave." Karan answered briefly without getting into any further discussion.

Kavya had already cleaned the puja room and decorated it well. She prepared gujia and got ghewar and peda delivered from the nearest sweet shop. Even though being on fast since morning and not a drop of water, she was full of energy and happy she was celebrating her first teej. It would have been wonderful and she would have felt so blessed if things were normal between her and Karan.

Kavya looked through her balcony, women had gathered on the ground for teej celebration. Kavya locked the door and moved to Smriti's apartment to take her along.

Kavya enjoyed the gathering and celebration in her society, but every now and then she looked at mobile phone for the time. Husbands too now gathered to join their wives in the celebration.

Kavya's restlessness wasn't hidden to Smriti. "He will come soon." Smriti tried to cheer her up but as much as she knew Karan, she could guess he may not even bother about this festival and the fast Kavya had kept for him.

Kavya came back home and lied down on the bed. It was seven and Karan wasn't yet back.

"Don't know why my family members are after me all the time. I am sick of all this," Karan said looking through the glass window, while Jia stood beside him. She had rarely seen Karan so annoyed. This marriage had absolutely destabilised his temperament. He used to be a very jovial and cool person and his witty side known to all. But many had noticed his mood swings. People who knew the reality would just ignore but those who didn't know the complications in his life would question to which Karan would simply smile away.

Jia gently put her hand on his shoulder and made him face her.

She looked into his eyes lovingly and planted a gentle kiss on his cheek. "Calm down. Your family would understand gradually that they can't force you into a relationship. It's not that simple." She said.

"Did I tell her to keep the fast? Is there a husband-wife thing between us? Then, why this melodrama? My mother called me in the morning, my sister called me later and then Kavya's mother too called me up - all trying to remind me the duty of a husband. Bloody hell, I am a donkey who is not supposed to hold any emotions, and anybody would come and kick me on my ass forcing me to do whatever they want." Karan's words seemed to be erupting like lava from deep inside his heart. Jia wanted to calm him down but before she could say anything, his cell phone rang.

Karan saw the name flashing on the mobile. "Now what does she want from me; to be back home on time?"

Karan reluctantly picked up the phone. "Yes". This one single word, the way it was uttered was enough to bring Kavya to shivers on the other side.

She mustered some courage and asked, "When will you be back home?"

"What do you want from me? Should I be packed inside the home immediately after office? Do I not have freedom to do what I want? Remember, I have a personal life of my own. And please don't intrude into that." Karan almost shouted on the phone. He had never talked to Kavya this way but today his mood wasn't his usual self.

A brief silence prevailed on the other side, later Kavya said in a broken and devastated, "It's eight thirty. I just wanted to know if you would have dinner at home."

"No, I won't have dinner and please stop worrying about me. I have never told you to wait for me." Karan disconnected the phone.

Jia had been watching him keenly while he was on phone. Karan was usually not this rude to anyone until something really went extreme. Whatever it was, Karan was her love and though she never expressed openly, she just hated that girl who had unexpectedly landed like anything into their life and so adamantly was trying to be his wife almost reducing her to the other woman. But Karan was all hers and so was his love. Yes, she didn't feel good even if Karan pitied for that girl and her innocence. But she knew that was just Karan's generosity which popped out anywhere even if he hardly knew a person. But today, Karan's attitude towards Kavya was something that amused her. She had never met Kavya but whatever she had known her through Karan she didn't find her innocent. If she was that innocent and cared for him, she should have by now taken a strong stance and freed him from her clutches. But no, she is constantly making effort to win him, but she would understand sooner or later Jia and Karan are inseparable.

Jia looked at Karan whose facial expressions remained the same giving a pissed off look. Jia held him by his shoulders and made him sit on a chair. She leaned over him and holding his face by both her palms, she came closer to him and whispered in a hushed voice, "Forget everything now. You are with me, your love. There is no one, just you and me…" Jia's lips brushing against his mouth tempted him for a smooch. She knew Karan could never resist her and she could turn his mood on pulling him out of the mood he didn't deserve to be. She was his wild fantasy! And she was right; Karan soon held her tight and pulled her to his lap; her legs crossing him on both sides and their mouths intensely grabbing each other. Moments later, they were on the bed lost in their world of ecstasy.

The clock struck ten and Jia and Karan still lied on the bed holding each other, nude and lost into each other.

"Karan let's have something. And yes, I have got a brand-new bottle of whisky for you," Jia winked pulling him out of the bed.

She warmed the seekh kababs that she had ordered from a food outlet and brought it on the table. She served Karan a drink, then another and then yet another and soon he had consumed more than he could sustain himself in his natural self. He usually was balanced whenever he drank but today when his sweetheart was offering him with a smile, he knew it was all to make him forget and overcome the pains of his complicated domestic life.

"I think I should stay back here tonight," Karan said in a shaky voice while his eyes were droopy.

Jia looked at the time on her mobile; it was eleven at night and then looking concerned, she said, "I think, today you should go home, Karan."

"But why? I want to be with you. Why do you want me to go back to her? Or is it because you too like others think it to be a festival where I should be with her. Do you also have some preaching to do now?

"Of course not. I would always want you to be with me and not return to that girl. But it's just to avoid any kind of further arguments from your family."

"But Jia, I am not in a state to drive back home."

"No worries dear, I would drop you home."

"You?"

"Yeah, of course." Jia replied with a smile as things were going as she wanted. There at his home would be Kavya. Till now she hadn't faced her but today all she wanted her to know and understand well that Karan was all hers and no one could separate them ever. She wanted Kavya to accept the reality that Karan and Jia were made for each other and their relationship remained unaffected despite that farce marriage (that's what she always called) and her forceful presence in Karan's life.

Jia held Karan's hand as he was too drunk to maintain his balance and she felt he needed her support to walk. They took the lift to the car parking.

Jia helped Karan sit inside the car. "Jia you are so nice…my love, be with me always. Don't leave me." Karan muttered his eyes half closed as he rested his head at the seat.

Jia bent a bit over him and kissed gently on his cheek. "I am always with you my sweetheart."

She drove the car towards Karan's apartment. Earlier she was a regular visitor to his place. Quite frequently she used to stay there overnight and at times for days but then, things had changed so much in the past eight-nine months.

Jia rang the bell while she held Karan by his arms as he still couldn't maintain his balance.

Kavya, who was in her night gown, opened the door. For a moment she was surprised to see Karan with a girl. But then she soon guessed it would be none other than Jia. She had happened to see a few pics of them that lay in a book which had fallen on the floor while she was dusting the bookshelf.

"Hi, I am Jia. Karan was with me at my place, but he was a bit too drunk. So, I thought I would drop him." Jia said keenly looking at Kavya as she almost scanned her top to bottom. She was no doubt pretty, tall and slim and her persona certainly had the charm to capture the interest of a man. Jia had heard about Karan's wife from some of their common friends and now seeing her; she knew she was getting jealous of Kavya. But then, her heart assured her of her love that Karan was a one-woman man and it was she and only she in his life.

Kavya moved aside to let them in and looked on as Jia took Karan straight to his bedroom. Karan had comfortably rested his hand around her waist while Jia's hand wrapped around his back holding his shoulder. Jia gently pushed the door to almost close it and there was hardly anything visible from outside the room.

Kavya closed the main door, pulled a chair in the living room and sat down thinking about them. She hadn't thought that she would face Jia this way. She was a stunning modern woman who carried confidence and grace and was absolutely a perfect fit for Karan. No doubt their chemistry was intense. Kavya had been seeing Jia's name inked on Karan's hand since the day of her marriage; that fateful day when they were knotted together despite him revealing to all about his love and so much begging to let him go. Now, seeing them together Kavya felt a strong sense of guilt rushing through her mind- they are so much in love, made for each other and their chemistry could give serious couple goals. She had intruded into their life, trying to separate those two souls almost ruining their peace. Looking at the bedroom's door which was closed enough not to let her see the two inside, she could feel the love and compassion Jia and Karan had for each other. What on earth was she doing in their life? And what did this festival of teej mean for Karan and her? Certainly nothing for Karan! The stark reality was known to her from the beginning but still she was moving on and the reason being Karan whom she had fallen in love with and wanted to do everything for him to make him happy. But she had suddenly collided with the reality and felt being slapped hard for all through ignoring it.

Kavya's heart screamed out loud. She got up from the living room teary eyed and moved to the kitchen to get herself a glass of water. She came out of the kitchen to find Jia standing in the living, perhaps she was waiting for her.

"Karan has slept. He never used to drink to this extent but since his marriage he has got into drinking quite often and today he was a bit too disturbed. He kept repeating that nobody understands his feeling. I just pray to god to keep him fine and free of any kind of emotional and mental stress." Jia said with a sigh and glanced for a while at Kavya. "I hope you know about me. He had always been open about our relationship to everyone and that's why inked me on his hand to make it clear to the world that our love can't be erased ever. He comes to my place every day straight from office. It's difficult for us to be away from each other. This marriage has snatched away his smile and changed him so much. People have started noticing and pointing out the change in him. At times I feel worried for him slipping into depression if I am not around. However hard everyone may try, Karan would know just one name 'Jia' and it would be good if everyone accepts this at the earliest. Nothing could ever change between us!" Jia said what she had wanted to for quite some time now.

She could notice Kavya's face turning pale and eyes welling up with tears. Though she had never wanted to face Kavya, but now she was finally relaxed, whatever she had planned worked well. It was enough of this pseudo marriage and a hollow relationship of husband and wife between Karan and Kavya. It had snatched away all her peace and had left Karan and her relationship in doldrums. She had to show Kavya the true picture so that she stopped even dreaming of a life together with Karan and playing a typical wife to him. Kavya's dejected and gloomy face gave her the satisfaction she had wanted; thankfully, all went according to her plan.

Jia left Karan's home while Kavya stood benumbed wiping off the droplets of tears that rolled down through the corner of her eyes. She was still on fast without a drop of water and she had to continue till morning. Though she was all fine for the whole day but now she felt tired and weak. She quickly took the support of the chair and sat down. She knew this sudden fatigue wasn't because of the fast she had observed but all because of that harsh reality that Jia had made her see all over again. This fast was useless and there was no sense to keep it. People would keep preaching but she should at least understand that it is going to do no good to either Karan or her. Surely, Karan would be pissed off with all this drama; for him anything done to force the relationship of a husband and wife would be no less than a sordid and annoying episode.

Kavya got up from the chair and slowly moved towards her bedroom. She lied down and closing her eyes made a futile attempt to get some sound sleep. A few hours ago, the eyes which had started dreaming of at least having her husband by her side while she worshiped for his long life, were left in tears with dreams shattered into pieces.

It was eight in the morning when Kavya draped in a red saree keeping pallu over her head performed all the rituals religiously as gathered from her mother to bring teej to a closure. But with what ever happened the previous night, her heart was torn apart. She was awake till late night pondering a lot over her life now and in future; what and how she would be doing to it. She had never thought so such and was just taking every day as it came despite knowing the fact that her married life was going nowhere. But her heart and mind had taken a strong decision now; something that was difficult, but she had to as all she wanted was Karan's happiness.

Kavya took the plate of prasad and kept it on the table covering it with another plate. Karan had perhaps got up as she could hear him from inside. He was probably on phone. Kavya went to the kitchen to make tea.

Carrying the tray with cup of tea, Kavya knocked at the door. She pushed the door a bit and moved inside. She placed the tray on the side table and she saw Karan bare chest just in his shorts. Jia had perhaps made him comfortable yesterday. Seeing Kavya inside the room, Karan got a bit conscious and lowered his voice. Kavya quietly came out of the room avoiding any further gaze at him.

Despite fasting for over a day, she wasn't feeling like eating. She just had little bit of poha that she prepared in the morning and kept sitting at the dining table. She brought her notepad and pen to finish up a short story she had been writing for a monthly magazine. Paper and pen had now become her best resort to pour down all her emotions which at times became difficult to burry inside.

Karan came out of the room and saw Kavya sitting at the table deeply engrossed into writing. With the aroma of the dhoop and then seeing Kavya in a saree, Karan understood she had completed the fast and the rituals for teej.

He had noticed her very quiet today and not with the usual smile while she offered him the morning tea. There was obvious reason to it. He had shouted on phone while she called him yesterday. But she didn't retort. And then she met Jia as well, something which even he hadn't thought that they could come face to face. But Jia is the truth of his life and it had to happen sooner or later. Somehow still Karan felt a sense of guilt for shouting at Kavya. After all, she was just doing something which all married ladies do and what she had been told by her mother and mother-in-law. He knew it was not just him but Kavya too had been getting calls and instructions from family on phone on how to perfectly celebrate the festival. He could have politely refused to be a part of all this, but he had lost his temper. Karan stood for a while looking at Kavya who didn't realise Karan was there in the room. Isn't Kavya suffering more than him? - Karan thought to himself. She had suppressed her grief inside. She had no one to emotionally fall back on. Their families thought everything was fine between them now as she never complained of anything, seemed always happy and content and he himself never talked to his family about her or their relation. Parul too thought that they had overcome the past; that's what he had got whenever he talked to his sister. She had been close to Kavya but Kavya chose not to share the truth to her as well. Anyways, he was with her in this whatever relationship not for a long time; so, Karan just thought of being good to her till they were formally and legally separated.

"What is there for breakfast today?" Karan asked her with a smile sitting at the dining table.

Kavya closed her notepad and kept aside. She quickly took a plate and served poha with green chutney. It was again something that Karan liked. Kavya barely ate poha at her parents' place but she had moulded all her eating habits for Karan.

She kept the plate in front of him and served some prasad in a separate bowl. "This is prasad…if you want to have." She said a bit hesitant unsure if he could fume again thinking of teej.

Karan took some prasad with both the hands one on another, touched it with forehead and ate it. Kavya saw him closing his eyes in regard while he touched prasad with his forehead. Thank god at least he showed respect to the prasad- she thought.

She served him water in a glass and was about to get up when he asked, "Writing something new?"

"Yeah, a short story for a monthly magazine," she replied.

"I guess, some time back also you had sent a story. Isn't it?"

"Yeah, it was published and was appreciated by lot of readers. Seeing the good response, the editor has asked me to write again something new." She replied feeling better talking of her work that had been appreciated.

"That's really good. Keep writing. Today everybody is in a rat race of job, money, luxury but its good you are doing something you love to and to satisfy your soul. Keep pursuing your passion." Karan said and could see his words bringing back the smile on her face that had turned dull. He was used to seeing her always with a smile at least whenever she faced him. But her smile had that hidden pain of the missing marital joy. Whatever it was she smiled only for him and because of him. He had understood this well now.

Karan had just finished his breakfast when his cell phone rang. The call was from his mother. He picked up and a smile instantly came to his face with the news he received.

"It's amazing. I knew they would say yes. Our Parul, after all has everything of a desired bride. This is a perfect match and I think we shouldn't delay now." Karan was exuberant to hear the news. He turned to Kavya and said, "Ma wants to talk to you. The boy's family has said yes to the proposal and wants an early marriage as the boy would be leaving for a three years assignment to Singapore and Parul would accompany him."

Kavya took the phone and talked to her mother-in-law

regarding the marriage preparations and then talking to Parul she said, "I think you should come here to do your shopping. Chandni Chowk in Delhi would be a good option to get your lehnga and sarees. Come with mummy and we would all do the shopping together. It would be really fun."

After a good discussion, it was agreed that Karan's mother and sister would come to Gurgaon, stay there for some days and do the bridal shopping at different places in Delhi and Kavya would go back home along with them for preparations. Later, Karan would take leave and too join them back home.

CHAPTER 12

"Bhabhi, I want to talk to you something," Parul said coming to Kavya in the kitchen who was busy getting dinner ready for all.

"Yes Parul, what happened?" Kavya said turning to her sister-in-law who stood there with fine lines of worries evident on her forehead.

"Are you and bhai not sleeping together in one room?" She asked with a raised eyebrow.

"But why are you asking this? Of course, we sleep in one room."

"Then why are your clothes lying there in the other room. And I see a few more essentials things of yours in that room…even the nightwear too! Why? Whenever I had asked you over phone, you always told everything was fine and you two have together moved on. So, what is this then?"

Karan was passing by near to the kitchen when he heard them talking and thought to wait and hear how Kavya was going to handle this.

"Parul, I had been cleaning the rooms and the cupboards yesterday. You know how these maids are. They just do their duty without bothering to clean the nook and corners and the areas that don't come straight in their way. I just kept the things in the other room while cleaning but couldn't place all of them back. I will do that now. And now you sit and relax. It's been hardly an hour or so mummy and you have come after a tiring journey. Take rest; I will soon join you all." Kavya said trying to clear all the doubts cropping up in her mind. Kavya could sense Parul didn't seem fully satisfied with her reply but she didn't say anything further and went back to the room. Today, the maid had taken off and she had been busy throughout the day in cleaning, shopping for groceries and veggies and lot of other titbits at home. She wanted to make everything perfect before her mother-in-law and Parul came. In all these, she forgot to shift all her belongings to Karan's room. She had shifted the dressing mirror with the help of maid a day before, arranged her books and a few daily wears but forgot her lingerie, most of her suits and many other things lying still in her room. And this had only brewed up suspicion in Parul's mind.

Karan remembered the day when he was abducted and forcefully made to marry Kavya and found her to be the most hateful person on earth. His hatred for her had remained even after knowing that she too had opposed this forceful marriage. But gradually living with her under one roof and knowing her better, he had understood she was a girl with a golden heart. Yes, he had to admit it. Whatever the situation may be, Karan had started respecting her for what she was and the way she carried herself. But all said and done, his destination was just one name and that's Jia.

Sitting in the terrace, Kavya talked to Parul and her mother-in-law about Parul's prospective groom, his family and lot of other things. Karan too joined them and Parul could notice her brother had certainly changed since she had last seen him at home or even till a few months back when she had talked to him on phone. He had lost his smile and his natural self when he was tied into the nuptial knot. But today he looked in a good mood and Kavya's presence certainly didn't put him off. He talked to Kavya as he normally talked to any other person. So, it meant things had improved between them and perhaps he had accepted Kavya as his wife. God bless them - Parul prayed from her heart.

"I feel like having coffee and popcorn." Karan said with a boyish excitement.

"No, no. You sit. I will make for all of us," Kavya said standing quickly.

"No, today it's me who will be doing the honours for you all. Anyway, I feel it's been ages since I last got into the kitchen to make something. Kavya, you sit; I will get for all." Karan paced towards the kitchen.

Sarita kept watching her son for a while, glad to see him getting back to life.

"I am so glad that you two have moved on together in your life. Things had been unfortunate and sordid but sometimes it all happens for good." Karan's mother said lovingly putting her hand on Kavya's shoulder.

"I would say bhabhi has been the best thing to have happened in bhai's life. I knew someday he has to understand this." Parul hugged Kavya and wished for her, "Always be happy. That's all we want for you two."

Kavya didn't want a ruckus or give sleepless nights either to her parents or in-laws and that's why she preferred not revealing the reality of her relationship with Karan. But what had happened to Karan? On the day of teej he was indifferent, reluctant and the same serious man she had seen since her marriage but then suddenly from the next day he was changed, a lot had changed in him. At least his attitude towards her had drastically changed. He kept happy usually, quite often asked her if she had her dinner when he came home late and on weekends offered her taking to the market for shopping or any other work she had. He had turned a nice friend to her, but it was that's it; nothing beyond that. Kavya easily concluded he was being sympathetic and most probably the guilt of being rude to her had turned him good to her.

"Now, all I want is a kid playing in our house. Kavya, I hope you soon give me my grandson or a granddaughter." Karan's mother said with hopeful eyes all stuck to her daughter-in-law.

Those words pinched Kavya to the core, making her heart sink. She knew it wasn't possible. But all she could do now is to silently keep the things going on as it was and wait for the right time to take the important step which would be good for both Karan and her; in fact, all for Karan.

It was eleven and Karan had already moved to his room. Seeing Parul doing something nearby, Kavya avoided knocking at the door and somewhat hesitatingly moved inside Karan's room.

She closed the door. "I think we have to sleep in the same room till mummy and Parul are here. They don't know about us and I think it's better to let it be like this. And don't worry, I will sleep in the extreme one end of the bed." Kavya suggested though unsure of Karan's reaction.

Karan nodded. "That's fine; we will manage till ma is here," Karan took to one side of the bed and got engrossed in a magazine that he had been reading.

Though initially feeling uncomfortable being in the same room with Karan, seeing him unaffected by her presence, Kavya too turned to one side and being too tired, she soon fell asleep.

"Karan, can't this be postponed for a couple of days?" Karan's mother stared at him as he did the packing.

"Ma, this is official. I told you. It can't be avoided. And moreover, it's just a matter of four days." Karan said glancing at her mother while keeping his stuff inside the trolley bag.

"But bhai, tomorrow is your first marriage anniversary. And as I have seen earlier, your organisation has been generous enough to provide leaves on special days of an employee. Somebody else can go in lieu of you and moreover you have good understanding with your boss. Request him at least." Parul said concerned.

"Parul, you think I haven't tried this. It's urgent sister. I can't help it and at this time, there is no one with my skills to handle the situation." Karan said almost done with the packing.

"But bhai…" Parul wanted to say something further when Kavya interrupted and said, "Parul it must be urgent, that's why Karan has to leave on such short notice. It's okay, we can celebrate later."

Karan's gaze turned to Kavya who just smiled as their eyes met. What a girl she was - he was forced to think again. Can on earth, there would be people like her who would selflessly and almost blindly support someone sacrificing all her desires and wishes - Karan thought to himself. That's what she always did. Her love for him was very much evident and known to him. He just felt sorry for her; there was hardly anything he could do for her except making her free of this marriage. This of course, he had planned for his own interest, but it was going to do good to her as well. She would be free of the clutches of this unwanted and unfortunate marriage and can move on in her life. This marriage had to end at all cost!

"And what about the shopping? Who will take us?" Parul asked not looking happy with her brother.

"Let me come back and then we would go wherever you want. But still I would say, it would be better if you guys take a taxi and go for shopping wherever you want. Men hardly have any role while women are shopping. Isn't it?" Karan grinned as he tried to convince his sister.

"I think that would be better. We would hire a taxi and go for shopping any day we want. If it is for Karan, then we have to wait till the weekend." Kavya too tried to convince Parul.

"That's superb. See Parul, Kavya has become very bold and independent now, doing things on her own. Girls should always be on their own rather than being dependant on a man. And moreover, I hardly have any idea about bridal shopping. You may take Smriti along with you. She has been living in Delhi NCR for a long time and is a good friend to Kavya."

"You don't worry Karan. We will manage. You focus on your work. If at all anything would be left out, we will shop once you are back," Kavya said trying to settle the matter.

Looking at Kavya, Karan just nodded with a smile.

Kavya stood in the terrace along with Parul and mother-in-law waving goodbye to Karan and wishing him happy journey.

"I will call once I land at Pune airport," Karan said waving at them as he got inside the cab.

Even though Kavya smiled seeing him off, she tried hard to control her emotions that waited to erupt. She had to. It was his life and she had no say in it. And no right to question him. She knew Karan wasn't going to Pune. Yesterday she had accidently happened to glance over the message that had popped up on his mobile while he was in other room. It was just a reminder for his flight from New Delhi to Goa. She could then gather all. Of course, when this marriage had no meaning to him, why would he bother for any celebration for anniversary? It was anyway better he went on a vacation with Jia rather than doing all those fake celebrations.

CHAPTER 13

As per the plan, after spending a couple of days at the residence of Karan's parents, Kavya came to her parents' house. It was after a year that she had come to her parental home since her marriage. She was overjoyed to meet all but despite being among her loved ones, she felt a void inside her and she knew why. Karan's face floated before her eyes even though she tried to push away the thoughts. Karan had come to see them off at the airport. Though he didn't say anything separately to her while saying random things to Parul and his mother, he did glance at her with a smile and that was to mean that his conversation also included Kavya. All she could think that she had so much become the object of sympathy to him.

Talking to her family members, Kavya somehow felt all wasn't well. Her uncle and father were not at home. Even Kundan and Raja weren't there. Till a couple of days ago all were so excited that she was coming home after a year but coming home, she didn't find that joy on the faces though she was welcomed home with all the rituals. Specially her aunt seemed devastated.

"Is everything fine ma? Why are you all so quiet? Where is papa and where's uncle? Papa was most excited to know that I am coming home. Now what is that so urgent that he is not present to meet me?" Kavya asked staring at her mother. Seeing her quiet, she turned to her brother, "Sundar bhai, will you say something now?"

Keeping mum for a while, he said, "Trisha is in ICU".

"What? What happened to her? And why did somebody not tell me anything earlier?" Kavya felt as if someone had hammered on her head. Trisha, her uncle's daughter, two years elder to her was the one whom she was very close to since her childhood. They had always shared all their secrets be it their crushes, their mischiefs, their dates or even their wild imaginations. Trisha had always been a lively girl till she got married. And later everything in her life had changed.

"She tried to commit suicide by slashing her wrist. By the time she was rushed to hospital, a lot of blood had oozed out." Sundar informed her.

"What? And when did it happen?" Kavya asked still struggling to grasp this piece of news.

"Yesterday."

"And why was I not informed? How is she now?

"She is out of danger, but doctors are working to bring her to a stable condition. We know you are very attached to Trisha and hearing this news could leave you disturbed. You had come to your in-laws' place after a long gap and we didn't want you to be upset." Kavya's mother said coming close to her.

"Family's pride, prestige, ego, that's what you all have always thought and cared for. Right? Also, you all claim to care for your daughters' happiness. Unfortunately, girls of this house have never been happy. You people can never understand where a girl's happiness lies. Trisha had always been so lively and strong but for the last two years, she was so broken from inside. And it's all because of you people. Sunder bhai, please take me immediately to the hospital. I want to meet my sister." Kavya said restlessly as

Trisha's face reeled before her eyes.

Kavya sat on a chair beside Trisha looking at her innocent face that had lost its usual sheen. Trisha had been shifted from the ICU as her condition was now under control. Kavya took her palm between her hands and pressing it affectionately said, "Trisha, why did you do this? Was this the only solution? Sister, your life is so precious to us."

Trisha couldn't say anything; just that tears trickled down her cheek.

Kavya wiped away the droplets wetting Trisha's pale cheeks and turning to her father, uncle and brothers who stood nearby, she said in voice tough and loud, "It's all because of you people. You all didn't let her marry the man she had loved just because she had dared to choose her life partner on her own and the boy didn't meet up to your standards. I still remember he was so mercilessly beaten by the goons sent by you and then you all chose the son of one of the richest men in town for Trisha ignoring the notorious reputation the males of the family had. Every male of that family is a womaniser and known for having mistresses and it's so ridiculous that they take pride in it! The whole town knows this, but no one dares to speak against them. You all too knew this, but you were hell bent on marrying Trisha in that family. Why? Because they are rich, powerful and you believed this marriage would bolster your political connect as well. You all forcefully made us believe that Trisha is going to have a fairy-tale life there. And now here she is. If this is the fairy-tale, God forbid such fairy-tale life to anybody." Kavya had never been so aggressive and loud talking to the elders of her family. She had been tamed not to revert to the male members of her family as they always took the right decisions for the house and its family members. She had been spectator to lot of things in the family that her heart never approved, but she remained quiet. But today her heart screamed out for her sister seeing her suffer so much emotionally, mentally and physically.

"By God's grace, my daughter is back home and all fine." Trisha's mother hugged her planting a kiss on her forehead. Looking at other family members sitting in the living she further said, "The best thing is that her father-in-law has regret for all that happened. He told that Trisha is precious for them and they are so lucky to have her in their family. They don't want to lose her at any cost. Even her husband has apologised for all that happened. He would be coming to take her along."

"What?" Kavya was utterly shocked to hear her aunt. She turned to her father, "Really, are we still thinking of sending Trisha back to that virtual hell? Do you still want to believe that they are going to take care of her feelings?"

Before Kavya's father could say something, her aunt roared like anything, "Kavya, what do you want - your sister's marriage to end and she should stay at her parental home forever. It was Trisha who started the argument with Vimal, she shouted at him. Which man would tolerate such behaviour from his wife? No woman behaves in such an absurd manner. He is a man, the bread earner, travels for his business, interacts with lot of people, and meets both men and women. That doesn't mean Trisha would start doubting his character. Constantly nagging would irk him and make him lose his temper. They have given her a luxurious life, lot of servants always at her beck and call, a car with a chauffeur ready to take her wherever she wanted. Vimal has taken her to foreign destinations for vacations. What else does she want? She should concentrate on having a child. That's going to strengthen her hold in that family with passing time."

Kavya kept staring at her aunt in disbelief. "Wow that's such a superb solution to all her troubles. Bear a child, be tolerant, shut your eyes, ignore whatever is going on and you are eligible to be blissful. Aunty, for god's sake she is your daughter! Trisha knows he has a mistress, whom he has kept in a separate apartment somewhere out of the town and perhaps she is pregnant with his child."

"Kavya, will you shut up?" Aunt shouted at the top of her voice.

At the same time, her father too rebuked her, "Will you stop blabbering? There are elders in this house to voice their opinions and take a decision. Getting married doesn't give you a certificate of maturity and interfere in matters where you shouldn't. We had taken a decision for you as well, but you opposed saying forced marriage is wrong, this and that. That time too you tried to preach us the ethics, the rights, the wrongs. But just look, you are happily married, your in-laws love you so much, Karan takes care of all your needs. You are having such a satisfying life! What else do you want?"

Every single word from her father seemed to be piercing through her heart forcing her to confront the truth of her married life. Her eyes got moist, voice choked, and lips dried up. She struggled to say, "There is nothing in my marriage." These few words were enough to turn heads and raise eyebrows. She continued, "Let me make you aware of the stark reality. There is nothing like a husband and wife between Karan and me. We sleep in different rooms. He has never touched me ever. It's his kindness that he hasn't behaved with me indecently ever, but I am no one to him. I am just a burden that he is carrying on till the time it would become unbearable for him. Jia is the love of his life and he had made it clear while you all were hell bent on forcing him to marry me. They are inseparable and made for each other. If ever he loses Jia or is forced to, I can bet he would lose his mental balance or even end up his life."

Silence prevailed in the room as everybody was all ears to the unexpected and shocking revelations.

"But Kavya, you never told this to us. Whenever we talked on phone, you seemed happy and spoke all good. Why didn't you tell us?" Her father seemed unwilling to accept the harsh truth.

"So that you could have sent your goons to threaten or beat up his family or even him. Right? That's what you all can think of. And you think that would have solved the problem. Just like you thought you won war of pride and ego by forcing Karan into marriage. You can never make your daughters happy rather you would slowly burry them to death." Kavya took a pause and said further, "Now let me make it clear. Don't ever interfere at least in my life. You have already spoilt it. Don't even think of doing the damage control now. Neither your guns nor your goons can scare me or Karan. I know what I need to do to my life. And if ever you try to harm Karan or his family, remember you are going to lose your daughter and before I succumb to death, I will stand against you for Karan and his family. Don't forget, I have the same blood running through my veins." Kavya left the room sending the shock waves to everybody present in the room making them gasp.

"Sarita, I must admit Kavya is a jewel. I have been watching her since couple of days, she has taken over all the responsibilities making you almost free of everything. Always the pallu on the head, so respectful to the elders, such well-behaved and treats Parul like her own sister. To top it all, she is well qualified academically. Now-a-days, you would hardly find girls who care for their in-laws genuinely." Karan's aunt who had come from Kolkata to attend Parul's wedding was highly impressed with Kavya.

"You are right, I really feel fortunate to get a daughter-in-law like her. God has been gracious. In fact, I would say God has blessed me with two daughters." Sarita replied feeling relaxed and contended.

A lady residing in the neighbourhood too joined them finding the discussion interesting. "Initially when we heard about Karan being abducted for marriage, we thought his life is now totally spoilt. Look at the notorious background of her family."

Sarita stared harshly at the lady and retorted, "The boy has married the girl and not her family. And moreover, they have given her good education, decency and culture. What else is required of a girl? As far as I know, your daughter is not even a graduate and had tried to run away with the son of that bakery shop owner. Right?"

The lady hadn't expected this befitting reply. Twisting her face, she immediately got up and moved away from the spot.

Karan who was sitting nearby watching the wedding rituals of his sister going on under the mandap was all ears to the conversation between the ladies. He just couldn't resist to grin at how his mother silenced the lady. And without an iota of doubt at least it can't be denied that Kavya had all decency, culture and mannerisms and without any exaggeration, he felt she was a perfectionist too. That's what he could gather in the last one year. Karan's eyes simply got fixed on Kavya. In a green and golden Banarasi saree, hair tied in a bun and a red rose adding to the hairdo, Kavya looked ravishingly beautiful. She was all along busy standing near the mandap and assisting the priest with whatever goods he required to carry out the wedding rituals. Parul had been so dependent on her for all her shopping which Kavya had perfectly managed. Everybody was all praise for her including Parul's in-laws. Karan was almost lost gazing at her before the priest called out the bride's brother and his wife to perform some ritual.

With moist eyes and heavy heart, newly wedded Parul was all set to leave her parental home. Holding her bridal lehnga from sides she slowly came close to Kavya and holding her hand pulled her a bit away from the crowd.

"Bhabhi, I know you have been hiding the truth from us, but bhai is still in a relationship with Jia. On marriage anniversary, bhai wasn't on any official tour but with Jia. I had heard her when I called up bhai to wish him. I am pretty sure you too were aware of this. Your face said it all. I know, it's so painful for a lady to see her husband with another woman. You are suffering without any fault of yours. You should think seriously of your life ahead as this is not how things should go on forever. But still my heart says, bhai and you are made for each other!" Parul hugged Kavya tight while Kavya too wrapped her arms around Parul who was, a true friend, an awesome sister and a staunch support in whatever short span of time they had been together.

CHAPTER 14

The clock struck two in the afternoon.

"I think we should have lunch now," Jia said looking at Karan while still lying in his arms. To this Karan tightened his grip around her puling her close to his bare chest. They had been lying on the bed for couple of hours now, sexually entwined and making love to each other.

"I don't feel like leaving you." Karan voice was still laden with sensuousness. "Life is so peaceful with you as if I have achieved everything and hardly any desire remains unfulfilled."

Jia's face turned a bit grave and then loosening his grip a bit, she said, "Karan it can't go on now like this. Your sister is already married. You need to now talk to Kavya regarding divorce and initiate the process. You know it's become so difficult to make my parents wait any further for my marriage." Kavya removed Karan's hand resting around her waist and got up from the bed. "Come let's have lunch."

Karan too got up, went to the washroom to freshen up and came to the table where Jia was serving chicken curry and rice. She had already cooked the food before Karan had arrived at her place. They had planned to spend this Sunday together and then Karan would be dropping her at the airport in the evening as she had to leave for Chandigarh to her parents' place for a couple of days.

"Jia, just give me a few more days. It's been hardly a week since we are back from the wedding. Parul would be leaving for Singapore with her husband in ten or twelve days. Though I can talk to Kavya even now and I really don't bother what her family's reaction would be, but I just don't want anything absurd or indecent to happen while Parul is still here. You know her husband's home is close and news spread like fire at our place. So, just give me some time; I have already planned how I should take this further and I believe I would be free from the clutches of this marriage soon and then without wasting any time, we would get married." Karan said looking intensely into Jia eyes.

Jia was contended with Karan's reply and both started with their lunch.

"There's great news Karan to share with you. Early morning my mother informed me that my dad has got a ticket from the ruling party to contest the state assembly election. And there's a strong belief that once again the ruling party would be back to power in Punjab. The seat from where my father would be contesting is also considered to be a stronghold of the party. The outgoing MLA is too old now to handle things. My dad had really worked hard to get to this," Jia was extremely excited to share the news with Karan.

"Wow, that's wonderful! So, now soon you would be the daughter of an MLA with bodyguards keeping an eye on you, the only daughter of the MLA. Hope they don't break my arms and legs seeing me so close to you." Karan was back with his humorous side with a grin.

"Who can dare to do that? You are my love, my life and soon we would be together forever." Jia said with a child-like vigour on her face.

"Love you baby. Your being in my life is all I need, and your love is the fuel that keeps me going."

CHAPTER 15

Karan paced restlessly in the premises of the office outside the main building. What had suddenly happened to Jia? Till the day before yesterday, everything was fine. What suddenly changed when she went to Chandigarh? Is she under the pressure or influence of her parents? They already had talked twice since morning and both times she wasn't in a good mood. The only thing she kept saying was to talk immediately to everybody including his and Kavya's parents that he was ending the marriage. All he wanted was some days of time as his parents, relatives and all known had barely come out of the joyful experiences of Parul's wedding. At Parul's in-laws' home, the post marriage celebrations had hardly ended. It was just a week when Parul had stepped into a new life where she was slowly getting accustomed to the new relations she would be living throughout her life. This was not the right time for him to declare his intent for separation from Kavya. If it reached Kavya's parents, it won't take much time to spread out to all the relatives and even Parul's in-laws. He had explained everything to Jia but still she has got back to square one and even adamant on it.

Karan had tried calling Jia twice in the last one hour, but she disconnected the call. Karan called her again and this time she picked up.

"Karan, what's the point of talking on the same matter again and again when you don't agree to this." Jia wasn't in a pleasant mood at all.

"Jia please understand; just give me some time. I told you divorce has to happen at all cost and I will initiate it soon."

"Karan, tell me something. Why you are always scared of taking a strong step? Earlier they forced you to marry that girl and you did. You couldn't revolt. Then even after marriage you should have reported to the police; that too you didn't. It's been over a year since you are with that girl. You told me to wait for your sister's marriage, I waited and now again you want me to wait. And then again you would say to wait till your sister has kids. What the hell is going on?"

"Jia, I couldn't do much to stop the unfortunate happenings all because I was worried about my family and their safety. Perhaps destiny at certain times is so strong that despite all your wishes, you can't change it. But good things do happen at its own pace and at the right time. You know well that how determined now I am to legally separate from Kavya and again I reiterate the same; I am going to do it. All I need is your support. Without you I stand nowhere." Karan's voice had turned emotional and somewhat choked.

After a silence for a while on the other side of the phone, Jia said, "Karan, I don't know why at times I feel you are slowly falling for that girl. You say you have sympathy for her, but I feel it's more than that. And if there is really anything such brewing in your heart, please do tell me. In that case, I would marry a boy of my parents' choice and there is no point waiting for you then."

"Jia what has happened to you suddenly? You know well, it's you and only you in my life. Just tell me something did you had talks with your parents on this matter and is it because of them that you have been behaving so absurd with me since yesterday? Somehow, I always felt your father had second thoughts about me; I was perhaps never his choice to be his son-in-law. He had reluctantly agreed may be because of you and now he is trying to create barriers between us," Karan said point blank.

This didn't go down well with Jia. "Will you now stop talking bullshit about my father? Every parent has second thoughts when their daughter selects a man of her choice to spend life with. That's natural when you care for your kids and with time everything becomes normal. I feel Karan, you need to relax and think about us seriously. I have already told you what I want and now you must decide if I really have a place in your life or it's just your family for you. Now, please don't call me till you have started with the divorce proceedings." Phone was disconnected.

Karan kept standing still for some time in the lawn and then paced back mechanically into the office's building with a gloomy face.

Kavya was surfing the channels sitting in the living while her mind was continuously pondering over something. Today she was all decided to talk to Karan something that had been in her mind for quite some time. Karan's happiness is all that mattered to her and she was certainly going to be out of his way. Kavya was deeply engrossed in thoughts when the doorbell rang. She opened the door and found Karan at the door. It was just six in the evening and Kavya hadn't expected him so early. Karan walked straight to his room and looking at his face, Kavya could guess all was certainly not well. He came home early only when Kavya wasn't there in the town. But that is no reason he would look so dull.

Kavya moved to the kitchen to make tea for him. Seeing it was snacks time and he would be hungry, Kavya quickly fried some onion pakoda and served them in a plate along with some green chutney. She had seen her mother-in-law cook this for Karan at times in the evening and Karan relished it with ginger tea. She loved doing these things for him but sadly, this wasn't to continue forever.

Kavya knocked at the door which was half closed and went inside taking then the tray with tea and snacks. Karan glanced at her and said, "Please keep it here."

Kavya kept the tray on the tool beside the bed. As she came out of the room, she could notice Karan lost and somewhat disturbed. On the family front, everything was fine. So, that couldn't be a reason to put him to worry. Workwise, she knew Karan was never stressed. Then what was the matter? Kavya had wanted to talk to him regarding the decision she had taken with respect to their marriage but seeing him not in a fine mood, she just thought of talking sometime later.

It was almost two hours since Karan came back from office, but he hadn't come out of his room. Kavya was making the dinner but since Karan liked hot chapatis straight out of the oven though he had never demanded that from her, Kavya just thought of checking with him when he would like to have the dinner. She went to his room pushing the door and was shocked to see Karan sitting with a bottle of whisky and a glass. He hadn't yet started but was perhaps about to. So, till then what had he been doing- just sitting on the bed lost for almost two hours? She hadn't ever seen Karan boozing at home. She had got to know from the maid that he used to drink at home occasionally along with Jia before marriage, but he never did that since she was with him.

"Should I serve dinner for you?" She asked.

"I don't feel like having."

"Little bit." She insisted.

"No, seriously I don't feel like. You please carry on."

Kavya didn't insist any further and just came out of the room gently pulling the door. Karan preferred the door to be shut enough to keep his privacy intact.

While quietly having her dinner, Kavya couldn't keep her mind off Karan. Why was he behaving so weird today? Something wasn't right with him. But what? Was it something related to Jia? Kavya felt like sitting by his side and with all the love and affection asking him what was eating him up from inside. Her heart was going all out for him seeing him in this state. She tried to hold on to her imaginations and control her feelings convincing herself that they are going to separate soon. Their paths are different, their lives are different, and they are no way meant to be together. But still some sort of magnetic attraction was tempting her to constantly think of him.

She cleaned the kitchen and switching off the light moved towards the terrace. The light in Karan's room was still on. She paced in the terrace still thinking of him. She knew she couldn't get sleep today till she saw Karan sleep peacefully. After walking in the terrace for a while, she pulled a chair and sunk into it staring at the stars right over her head in the sky. A web of thoughts kept her mind working. There were no strings attached between Karan and her but he treated her well, took care of her day to day needs – (of course not the physical one which though at times she so much wanted), took her out to some mandatory parties (as those required spouse to be present), gave her pocket money to run the house and she had indeed started feeling like being Mrs. Rai. And it was such a wonderful feeling even though it was short lived.

Suddenly she heard a sound from Karan's room, of some glass breaking down. Kavya ran towards the room.

"It's all fine. Just that the glass slipped from my hand," Karan said as he staggered and struggled to stand. He took the support of the bed and sat down with a bit of thud.

Kavya could see Karan had already emptied the bottle. The glass pieces were scattered on the ground. "I will clean the floor." Kavya collected the pieces and cleaned the floor. After cleaning her hands outside in the washbasin, she came back in.

"What happened? Is there any problem? I have never seen you drinking at home." Kavya asked concerned, looking straight into his eyes. After gulping the whole bottle of whisky, he was certainly not into his complete senses but not even totally out of his mind.

Rather than replying her back, Karan kept staring at her with a gentle smile at his face. He got up and came close to her. Then further closer. Kavya at first got conscious as what he was upto, but his face had the softness, his lips played a gentle smile and his eyes had the depth that could even melt her inside him.

Karan held her hand and brought her close to the bed. "Sit here," he said and sat by her side, his fingers almost touching hers. "You know something Kavya, you are a very sweet girl; so loving, so caring. I am sorry for being rude to you many a times. But you know Jia and I love each other and had always wanted to be together. This marriage jolted me from inside. But I know it was no way your fault. You did your bit to stop the marriage but girls back there in our male dominated society hardly have a say. You kept doing the duty of a wife selflessly, taking care of even my slightest of needs. And my parents aren't tired of appreciating you and talking of you to all and one they meet. My sister is your biggest fan. Relatives, my colleagues, even my closest friends Sumoy and Maya- they all have nice things to say about you. What a girl you are? Whoever meets you becomes a fan of yours. And yes, I know you love me, and I feel really fortunate to be loved by someone who is such a wonderful person." Karan said, taking pauses while eyes seemed heavy with intoxication.

Kavya's eyes got moist and tears trickled out through the corner of her eyes as she listened to those words that just touched her heart. She had never seen this side of Karan. But people say you blurt out truth when you are drunk. Even though the path ahead was going to be tough, these words from the man she loved will always stay locked inside her heart as biggest treasure of her life.

Karan continued, "But Jia has suddenly stopped talking to me. She knows it well that she has been the only woman in my life and she is my heart, my soul but still she tells I am not serious about our relationship. I told her at right time, things will be good again and we will be together again forever. I just needed some more days of time to start the divorce proceedings. Parul has just been married and I wanted some time to things get settled before I let everybody know this."

Kavya was dumbstruck. So, it wasn't just she thinking of telling him about divorce, Karan too had planned for this. So, things are sorted but why this is painful and pinching her heart? She once again consoled her bleeding heart- this is what she wanted too, and it was all just for Karan, the only man she had ever fallen in love with!

"Should I bring some lemon water for you? You would feel good." Words struggled to come out of her throat. As she waited for his reply, she found herself under his warm and affectionate gaze. Her eyelids dropped down as she couldn't hold herself to those eyes so close to her almost hypnotising her. Sitting close to Karan, she hadn't been in such a situation ever. She could sense, he was still looking at her.

"No, I don't need that," he said his eyes transfixed on her. He held her by her shoulders and turned her towards him. "You are a beautiful soul and I know you love me. Believe me at times, I feel so fortunate that someone loves me so selflessly without any expectation, without any demand. Such selfless love really exists!"

Karan bent slightly and kissed her cheek as Kavya felt a sensation run through her spine. She shrugged for a moment thinking if she should stop him but then his lips came down brushing through her mouth giving her another electrifying sensation which made her forget any inhibitions that had crossed her mind. She loosened herself as his firm masculine arms tightened his grip around her. His mouth thrust on hers parting away her lips and as his tongue went all out to explore the pleasure, Kavya found herself giving up to him. Karan pulled her up and made her lie down comfortably on the bed and slowly peeled off her night gown and then her innerwear that lay down on the floor. Within moments he too was without a piece of cloth, mounted on her and Kavya pressed beneath his hard, masculine frame. Karan kissed her passionately all over her face as he also murmured - you are stunningly beautiful. His hand reached out to the switch to turn off the light and then again, he kissed her hard on her lips. He again murmured in a husky voice – I need you Kavya. Kavya felt melting down as his kisses grew intense going down her lips to her neck, her breasts and then all over her body.

Two souls whom destiny had plotted to be together, who had defied this fate, wanted to part their ways, were now skin deep into each other, moaning and forgetting everything else that lay outside these passionate moments.

Couple of hours later, Kavya suddenly got out of her sleep only to find herself lying in Karan's arm; his other arm wrapped around her waist. She slowly got up removing his hand from her waist and slipped into her night gown. Standing by the side of the bed, for a moment she glanced at the man who had given her memories of the lifetime that she should preserve as her biggest fortune. She leaned a bit and gave him a peck on his cheek. She knew she wasn't going to live these moments again. This was once for all but then his words still rang in her mind - "I need you Kavya". A part of her said it was just a slip of tongue and was surely meant to be Jia. She covered Karan who was deep into sleep without a piece of cloth on his body with a sheet.

Kavya was back to her room but sleep was far away from her eyes. Those treasured moments with Karan made her blush with satisfaction, completeness and the feeling of now being a woman!

Karan's hand moved out to fetch his mobile phone that was lying on the tool. It was seven thirty in the morning and he realised he could be late to office. The moment he wanted to get up and removed the sheet, he felt some heaviness as if something too bulky had been placed on his neck making it difficult to move. He remembered he had drunk too much previous night. He pressurised his mind a bit and it didn't take much time for him to understand and then recall what all happened yesterday. He held his head with both his hands almost cursing himself. How could he do that to Kavya? And then a sense of guilt overpowered his mind blaming himself - I cheated on Jia? And what would Kavya think of me?I never gave her the status of my wife in any way and now when Jia is out of town, me being drunk, brought Kavya to bed and did all that I wasn't supposed to. Holy God! What do I do now?

After pondering restlessly, Karan thought it best to talk to Kavya directly on this matter. After all, it wasn't just his fault. He hadn't forced her into anything. It was their mutual interest that brought them together yesterday. But now, he had to make it crystal clear about his plan of filing for divorce before the situation became complicated or Kavya drew some other conclusion after all that happened last night.

Karan took a shower and got quickly ready for office. Though he had so much wanted to take an off today because of the hangover but he didn't want to face Kavya for the whole day. The guilt persisted in his heart and he just wanted to be free of that.

Karan came out to dining table where Kavya had arranged the breakfast and was just waiting for him. Their eyes met, and Karan found it a bit difficult to stand up to her gaze. As usual, she looked like a breeze of fresh air, bathed early morning, dressed into a salwar suit, sindoor into her parted hair, a red bindi adorning her forehead and she stood with a smile to welcome him to the new day.

"Good morning," she said with the usual pleasant smile playing on her face.

Karan pulled a chair and sat down avoiding a look at her. Kavya served him omelette and the multigrain bread sandwich. She took care there was a change in his breakfast everyday as that was one meal, she was sure he would have at home.

"Please sit, I need to talk to you," Karan asked her upon seeing her standing by his side.

She took the chair beside him and her heart got pounding in the anticipation of what he was going to talk. He looked grave and perhaps had been mulling over yesterday night's incident.

"Kavya, whatever happened yesterday was unintended. I know I shouldn't be giving an excuse of being drunk and out of mind and control but to be true that was it. I don't know what happened, but I am extremely sorry for that. I would request you to forget it as a mistake and bury it such deep that it can't be remembered again. I may sound like a rogue and an utterly selfish creature but it's better to mend the things now rather than create complications later. Kavya, you know how much I love Jia. My life without her goes nowhere. I have already decided to file for divorce and I had wanted to talk to you regarding this. I know you are sensible, and you can understand my feelings. Rather than spoiling our lives, its better we separate and take on our new beginnings. You are a fabulous girl and I am sure you would find a perfect life partner. Your family would blast like anything knowing this but now nothing is going to hold me back. If there is a life, it's going to be with Jia." Karan said straight and upfront without a pause. He guessed it might be tough for her to hear this, but it had to come to her sooner or later.

So, here it was - the fact of their relationship and its end. After all, how long would she live in a mirage - Kavya thought. Her virtual world of wedlock had to collapse like a house of cards and it did. Anyways, she was prepared to it. She knew he was waiting impatiently for her reply.

"First of all, Karan - there is nothing you should feel sorry about. I too was a part to it and you didn't force me into anything. And you need not explain me how much you and Jia love each other. I fully understand how tough it is to even think of a life without the one who means the whole world to you. In fact, I too had wanted to talk to you about it. I want you and Jia to be together forever. Please start with the divorce proceedings; it will have my full support. And yes, don't worry about my family. They can't do any harm to you or your family. Take my words, I would handle all. I quietly gave up a year back; that was my biggest fault but not again." Kavya spoke in one breath and took a deep sigh. She bent down her head thinking of her own life without the man whose mere presence would make her bloom like a flower.

Karan saw the usual soft, submissive and shy girl now as tough, confident and determined. No doubt she had a lot of colours to her persona and that's what made her likeable to all. The respect for her multiplied in his heart and he silently saluted her.

The news that Kavya received from Sunder tore apart her heart making her burst into tears and cry out loud. No, Trisha can't do this - she tried to console her heart, but it was difficult for her to believe her body was to be cremated tomorrow. They were all waiting for her; she meant a lot to Trisha and she was the only one who had always supported Trisha whenever she spoke her heart and had begged all to listen to her.

Karan who had been relaxing in his room after being back from office came out in the living hearing Kavya sob so badly. "What happened Kavya?" Karan asked, worried to see her in such a state.

"My cousin Trisha is no more. She took poison and they

couldn't save her." She replied in a heavily choked voice as words struggled to come out. "

"Oh God, so sorry to hear this! But why? I guess she was married in a rich business family?"

"If just riches could bring all the happiness, then my sister sure would have been alive. Nobody cared for her feelings ever. Her heart had cried out loud when the man she loved had been beaten black and blue, his legs fractured and warned by our brothers not to ever come her way. Trisha was married without her wish to this rich brat who could never keep her happy. That bastard kept sleeping around with women. Every time Trisha wanted to explain her situation at our home, she was suggested different ways to keep her man happy and satisfied. It's barely a month when she had cut her nerve and was hospitalised but thankfully saved, she attempted suicide again. Knowing she was unable to fight, perhaps even God wanted to free her of this brutal world," Kavya's heart pained as Trisha's face reeled before her eyes; she kept sobbing as an unrestricted thick stream of tear rolled down her cheeks. "Trisha, my sister you shouldn't have given up. There was a life beyond it. We together would have fought." Kavya sat down on the sofa with a thud, holding her head with both her hands as her tears kept running down wetting her hands.

Karan too was shocked to hear the sad news. But he couldn't ignore the fire in Kavya against the family and the society she came from, where girls' wishes hardly mattered to anybody. When it came to the matter of their divorce, he could guess she was strong and tough on how to break the intent of her divorce out to the world and now perhaps tougher after this incident. She was going to clash with her entire family on her thoughts, her decisions and everything that mattered to her.

"I will book flight ticket for you. Should I come along with you?" Karan asked.

"Just book an early flight for me. No, I don't want you to come. I think I need to discuss lot of things with my family and you being there may turn the situation sour."

Karan nodded and took out his laptop to book a ticket for her. A morning flight was booked.

It was half past twelve at night. Karan came out of his room to take a bottle of water when he noticed Kavya sitting in the terrace her face grief stricken, her palms wiping away the droplets that lay below her eyes. Karan heart felt like going close to her, sitting with her and supporting her in this hour of pain but he held himself back - wasn't he too the reason for her pain? Yes, their separation was going to add up to her miseries and there wasn't anything he could do to that.

Days passed since Trisha's body had been cremated, but Trisha's memories had gripped one and all in the family snatching away the peace and joy from their lives. Trisha's in-laws were back to their normal life and murmurs of another marriage for their son had already starting floating around. This wasn't going down with anyone in Kavya's family.

"Bloody mother fuckers, it's hardly been a few days since Trisha left us and they are planning of another marriage. Let the police investigate the case. I want to see them all behind the bars."

Raja, the youngest of the lads in the family burst out in anger.

"Someone, please bring my daughter back…" Trisha's mother was simply unstoppable beating her chest with both her hands titling from one side of the chair to other while Kavya's mother stood by her side trying to control her.

"They have already given a counter statement and cooked up a story blaming Trisha's character. They have been telling that she was into an extramarital affair with her ex and when her husband caught her red handed and threatened to expose, she committed suicide." Kavya's uncle gave them the latest update on the matter, shocking all to the core.

"Such scoundrels! They have gone down to this level. Now, we will show them the worst side of us. Kundan, Raja take out the guns, it's time we show them out what we can do." Sundar roared, his eyes turning red and voice harsh and powerful enough to give a panic attack to anyone not used to it. "Viru, call our men and take out the cars. Soon! There will be bloodshed now. Nothing less than that." He shouted at the servant who was ready at his master's call.

"Cut off Vimal's head and bring it to me. I would drink his blood and that could only give peace to my daughter's soul. It's because of that bastard I lost my daughter." Trisha's mother said fuming and wiping her wet eyes at the same time.

Seeing her brothers come into action holding the guns, Kavya who had been a mute spectator and listener to all, shouted fiercely, "Will you all stop this? You think guns, bullets and bloodshed is the solution to all the problems. That's what you all have been doing and you think you have killed a problem, but it only bounces back creating a bigger problem for all of us. That's what you did beating up that guy Trisha was so madly in love. Couldn't that be avoided?

No! You try to be God to all in the town but forget there is the real one sitting up watching you all. Your karma would always fall back on you. My sister would have been so happy had someone understood what she wanted. You people didn't care for her pains and feelings when she had tried to end her life earlier. That time too you all preached her to be patient and keep her husband happy. She only wished not to go back to that hell again, but you all forced her and the poor girl gave up. You don't deserve her. You don't deserve a daughter in your family." Kavya stopped for a moment as all looked at her aghast but she had more to say. "Aunty, what kind of a mother are you who could never understand your daughter's feelings and now you are asking your son to behead someone because that would rest her soul in peace. Did you ever understand what her soul wanted? And what would you do if in this blood game you lose your son too? For God's sake, I once again request all of you please don't do this. We would take this matter to court; we will fight and let everyone know why our Trisha had to resort to suicide."

Silence prevailed in the room as Kavya's word kept hitting everyone hard forcing them to think and rethink what all she said.

"I think Kavya is right. Bloodshed is not the solution. We will fight in a legal way. And let's admit, it's our fault too. I still remember Trisha had begged repeatedly to let her marry that boy and then again to spare him and then yet again to not get her married in that family and every time we all turned a deaf ear to my daughter. Trisha, please forgive us!" Trisha's father couldn't hold his emotions and cried out for his daughter.

Virendra Sharma who had been quiet till now ordered the boys, "Keep the guns back. Nobody is going anywhere. Nobody is going to even touch the gun without my permission. I lost my father in a battle of ego that could be easily avoided. My mother died of heart attack on hearing the news. I lost my elder sister in honour killing, we took lot of lives too and then we lost our Trisha. Violence and ego will certainly not help anyone just that it would leave void and repentance in our lives." Turning to his daughter, he said, "Kavya, I have realised we are your culprit too. All we thought was kidnapping Karan and forcing him to marry you was going to settle our score with the family and yes, we did live in a fake prestige and pride that no one can even dare to go against our wishes. I admit we were wrong. Feelings, emotions and love can't at all be forced. Please forgive us daughter and let us know if we can be of any help to you ever." His voice was laden with guilt; the guilt of losing his niece and ruining his own daughter's life.

Kavya came near to her father, taking a deep breath, she said, "I want a divorce from Karan and that's what he too wants. He has already talked to the lawyers and the proceedings would be initiated. Karan and Jia are inseparable. They want to marry and spend their lives together and I don't want to be a culprit separating two souls. Moreover, I have already told you Karan and I don't have any relation that of a man and wife. He would die or lose his mental balance if he doesn't have Jia in his life."

"You know what you are saying Kavya? You want divorce? Has anybody ever even thought of it in our family?" Sunder interrupted.

Before Kavya could reply her brother, her father stepped in and in his baritone, said, "I wish we would have thought about it earlier, our Trisha would have been among us. There should be a first time to everything. Kavya, my daughter I am with you in all your decisions. You do whatever you feel right and never get worried of anything; your entire family is standing with you."

Kavya hugged her father as her eyes got moist but she was

thrilled to see the change in her father. The only regret was that this change and realisation in the family came after losing a near and dear one but time can't take a reverse gear.

CHAPTER 16

Kavya impatiently looked at the wall clock. It was just quarter to seven in the evening and Karan won't be coming anyway before ten at night. He would go to Jia's place after office, spend time there and then would be back late night. Kavya grew restless as she wanted to talk to him, face to face. Though she could talk to him in the morning, but he would be too busy getting ready for office and she didn't want to upset him with the news to spoil his entire day. No way could this news brighten his mood, that's for sure. But she had to let him know. Kavya remained perplexed rubbing her hands and constantly looking at the clock. Just then, the doorbell rang.

She opened the door and to her great relief, it was Karan. Karan seemed to be in a brilliant mood today. Perhaps his presentation with the top management went well, Kavya thought to herself. At times he used to tell her a bit at the breakfast table about the happenings in his office.

"Kavya, I am going out for a Sufi Night with Jia. It would get late. You have your dinner and sleep." Karan seemed in a hurry. Keeping his bag on the bed, he moved to the washroom.

Kavya moved to the kitchen to prepare ginger tea which Karan enjoyed when was at home in the evening. Kavya brought the cup of tea to the table where Karan was wearing his shoes. He had freshened up and changed into casuals.

"That's so nice of you Kavya. I really needed this ginger tea."

Kavya hadn't felt so nervous ever in her life. She was unsure how to start the conversation, but this was important and couldn't be avoided. She held her heart, mustered some courage and said, "Karan, I want to talk to you something important."

"Yes, please tell." Karan turned to her.

"Karan, I am pregnant."

An eerie silence prevailed in the entire room.

Karan looked blank at her, aghast as if someone had dropped bomb in the area. "What?" He still couldn't believe that!

"Yes, I had missed out my period and when I tested today with the kit, I found it positive. I never thought that just one single day could put me to this."

What the hell? Everything had been going smooth. The divorce process had started though much to his parents' dismay, Jia was happy, and the lawyer had said that process would be smooth without any hurdle. Now, when everything was so perfect, where on earth this problem cropped up from? Karan felt like scratching his head. "I really don't know what to say. I never thought, my one single mistake could create this trouble. This needs to be aborted." Just then Karan received a call from Jia. "I am just coming baby, will reach in another 15 minutes." Karan tried to sound normal on phone though he was shaken from inside.

It was eleven by the time Jia and Karan were back from Sufi Night. Karan had sent a text message to Kavya informing he would be staying back at Jia's place. He wanted to let Jia know about

Kavya's pregnancy. They were going to have a new beginning to their life and he didn't want to start it keeping a secret lifelong. He just hoped Jia understood him.

Jia had freshened up and got into her short lacy nightwear. Seeing Karan sitting on the couch somewhat worried and contemplating, she came to him and sat by his side wrapping her arms around his shoulder.

Kissing him gently near his earlobe and bringing her lips close to his, she asked in a sensual voice, "Why is my sweetheart looking so worried when I am here to take care of him?"

"Jia, I need to talk to you something." Karan muttered.

"What's that so serious that I couldn't turn your mood on?"

"Jia…" Holding her hands and looking deep into her eyes, Karan muttered again but couldn't utter a word beyond her name.

"Yes Karan. Is there something unnerving you? Speak."

Karan gathered some courage and said, "Jia, Kavya is pregnant."

"What?" These words came as a shock to Jia.

"Listen to me and please try to understand. It happened the night when you were in Chandigarh and in no mood to talk to me despite me requesting you so many times. I explained my situation, but you were so rude to me that day and even cut off my phone calls. You even went ahead saying that you would marry a boy of your parents' choice as there was no point waiting for me. You know that had shattered me fully and going back home I got drunk so much that almost lost my senses. For me, it was just you everywhere and even Kavya seemed to be you and just you. And that's when I committed the mistake of my lifetime. Jia, please forgive me for that. I love you unconditionally and believe me it was unintentional. I would ask her to abort the pregnancy. My life has been like an open book to you and there isn't a thing from my life that is hidden to you. I wanted you to know this as well as I couldn't spend my life with you carrying that guilt forever." Karan was all apologetic, soft and relieved as he explained her whole situation.

His eyes were fixed on her, desperately waiting for her response. She was quiet, looked away for a while and then getting up from the couch got herself a glass of water. Keeping the glass on the centre table, she got settled on another couch but was still quiet and her face had worn the silence of a graveyard.

It was getting difficult for Karan to withstand her silence; it seemed to be eating him up like termite. "Jia, please say something." Karan's restlessness was evident.

"Do I have anything to say, Karan? Is this a Bollywood story that you have narrated me? First, how could you sleep with that girl? Isn't it a superb excuse that you were drunk and couldn't figure out whom you were having sex with? Just because you were unable to suppress your sexual desire and for the whole world and that stupid, no, no - cunning girl, you are her husband and have the license to bring her to bed, both of you satiated your desires. As simple as that! She is still your legally wedded wife and I am just the other woman. That's the status I have gained since your marriage. Isn't it, Karan?" Jia's words came out like fire. She was no way convinced with the explanation Karan had provided her.

"Jia, what has happened to you? You are you behaving with me as if you have never known me. Have I ever eyed any other women except you? Have you ever heard about me involved in any flings, any flirts or any such act of mine that would make you rethink about my character? And where does this sexual desire thing come into picture? You know we have a very active and satisfactory sexual life. And Jia, do you doubt my character? It's you and only you in my life my love."

"Karan, why didn't you tell me when this happened? Why now when you got to know she is pregnant?" Jia had calmed down but still not convinced.

"Fear! Fear of facing you when I knew I was guilty and the anticipation of your harsh response, your wrath and a fear of even losing you. You know I can face the toughest of circumstances but not a situation where you have parted away from me. Moreover, I had talked to Kavya the very next day. I apologized to her and made it very clear that we need to bury that incident and move on thinking it was a blunder never to have committed or even thought of. But this news of pregnancy really shocked me to core and this wasn't something I would like to cover up and keep as a secret to you. You needed to know this. That's all I can say in my defence." Karan sounded low and disappointed.

Jia took a deep sigh and said, "Karan, give me some time to come out of all this. And I am sorry for being hard on you. You know dear, I can't share my love with anyone."

Jia's words brought an instant smile on Karan's face. He hugged her, caressed her and whispered into her ears, "I am all yours and thanks my love for your faith in me."

Kavya sat down on the couch holding her waist and closing her eyes for a moment. Her face looked dull, down and out.

"Still having cramps?" Smriti asked sitting by her side looking at her concerned. "I think you should call Karan. He is away from home for almost two days and here you are suffering to abort the pregnancy. After all, he too was responsible for this."

"It's okay Smriti. I am fine now. I think medicines have worked well. Tomorrow once again we would visit the gynaecologist for a final check-up. And thanks so much dear for all your support."

"Always for you sweetheart. At times I feel pity for Karan, he is losing out on a gem. But where is he? Shouldn't he be here with you?"

"He had been with Jia over the weekend. Would be coming home today evening after office. Moreover, he doesn't know that I had planned this abortion in these days." Taking a pause, she continued, "Smriti, I need another help from you. I want to take up a job as a school teacher. I need to be financially independent now as I am planning to move out of this house. Since, you are in the same profession, you can help me out with your contacts."

"I think this is a perfectly wise decision. You are a gold medallist, intelligent, smart and I am damn sure you would land up with some superb offer. I would try to find some good opportunity for you. Rest, I sincerely wish that you get all the happiness you deserve. I am leaving now but just give me a call if you feel uncomfortable or need any help." Smriti pressed Kavya's shoulder with all the affection and concern and that smile on her face assuring her that everything going to be fine in her life.

Standing in front of the dressing mirror, Kavya gently wiped off her wet hair with the towel and then as usual applied sindoor and a red bindi. The black beads of her mangalsutra seemed to be shining brightly and her love for bangles made her change them almost every day, going with the attire she chose to wear. She kept standing looking at her mirror image, keenly glancing over each and everything on her body that adorned her, that every married woman took pride of and all those that gave her the status of a wife to her mister. She so much loved these, dreamt of this right from the age she got to know what marriage was, looking at her mother and her aunt how much they treasured these but unfortunately her companionship with these was temporary. Sooner or later this tag of Mrs. Karan Roy was going to be snatched away from her. Kavya forcefully jerked away those thoughts and moved towards the kitchen to get herself breakfast and a cup of tea. Today Karan had left for the office a bit early and she too got late as she had been awake late night applying to a couple of schools. Though she had already been selected in a good one, but the offer letter was still awaited. By the time she got up in the morning Karan had already taken a shower. She somehow hurriedly prepared tea and bread toasts and omelette for him.

While having her breakfast, she just wished she got the offer letter from the school. It was a big international day cum boarding school. They were offering a good package and residence for teachers if they wished, inside the school campus. It was located at a distance from the hustle bustle of the main city of Gurgaon. Kavya almost begged God for this offer; she needed it desperately.

Finishing her breakfast, she opened laptop to check her mails. She had been regularly doing this since she was on to the job-hunting spree. To her excitement and heartfelt joy, there was the offer letter lying in her mail box. The authorities had mailed her the previous evening. She had been offered the job of a Hindi teacher along with the residence inside the campus. Kavya quickly picked up her phone and called up Smriti. She knew Smriti would be at her workplace and might be busy but she just couldn't hold her excitement.

"Hello dear, there's good news to share with you." Kavya chirped like a child.

"You got the offer letter?"

"Yeah."

"I knew. Who can be more deserving than you? Congratulations sweetheart. Now forget everything else and fly high."

"Thank you Smriti. It could happen all because of you. I would always be grateful to you for your support."

"Never say that again. You are a dear friend. I just informed you about the opening and rest it was all your effort. I had told you - they can't get a more deserving candidate than you. When is the joining?"

"Next week."

"Have you informed Karan about it?"

"I had told him some days back that I am looking out for a job and soon will be quitting the apartment."

"What did he say?"

"Nothing. That's what he and Jia want that I should shift as soon as possible. After all Karan and me are getting divorced."

"What about your families? They aren't doing their bit to stop you people from getting separated!"

"My family is with me and have given me all the freedom to take decisions of my future. As for Karan's family, they have been repeatedly trying to convince us, but Karan has almost stopped talking to them after getting irritated. Parul calls me from Singapore quite frequently and every time she hopes there's some change in our decision, but she too knows it's all upto her brother and for him, Jia Arora means the whole world. Even my parents-in-law came here, stayed with us for some days and did all they could to convince Karan. You know that; you met them. But I always knew, these are all futile attempts. I feel people should now come to terms to the reality and accept that Karan and Jia have a life together and not away from each other."

"I don't have to say anything on this but somehow I feel lot of good things are in store for you." Smriti said with a sigh.

"You carry on now with your work. I have already taken too much of your time," Kavya said and the conversation between the two ended.

Just one more week to go and she would be leaving the house. She looked around with moist eyes, the mini garden she had made in the terrace, the curtains that she had colour synced with the wall, the beautiful paintings and the bright colourful lamps that artistically adorned the rooms of the apartment. She seemed to have breathed her life into the house. She was going to miss everything and above all the man who dwelled in her heart while her heart simply refused to let him go even though she was going to move on in her life.

CHAPTER 17

Karan shut his laptop and came out of his cubicle to the break area somewhat annoyed. He took a cup of coffee from the blending machine and stood near the glass window of the break area. He sipped coffee looking out through the glass into the sky, his senses questioning him repeatedly - why is it happening so? It had been over a month now since Kavya had left his home but every time he went home, her memories haunted him like anything. First few days it was an utter chaos for him. He didn't know when the maid came in the morning and went away after ringing the bell. He couldn't even get up from his sleep to open the door. The cook, whom Kavya had arranged before she shifted, came late and Karan had to just compromise with plain bread and butter. He so much missed the ginger tea that Kavya used to offer him early morning with a pleasant smile on her face. And now he knew it made his mornings though his brains tried hard to negate his feelings, but it was true.

The other day cook had prepared the ginger tea for him, but Karan could never find that flavour. For initial few days, he wore the neatly ironed clothes that Kavya had arranged in his cupboard but later he had to give all his shirts and pants to the boy who ironed clothes for many of the families in the society. But then for that too, he had to find out time to go to him either on weekends or in the evening. The taste he had found in the food that Kavya prepared like his mother, he knew was unmatched. The dishes, the way of preparation, the usage of spices all that was specific to the place and state he belonged to and was used to right from his childhood, he could never find in any restaurant. While with Jia, they usually ordered from outside and at times Jia would prepare Punjabi kadhi with rice or chicken with rice but certainly this wasn't the food that he missed. Karan then remembered the Tulsi plant that Kavya had nurtured in a pot in the terrace. She used to water it daily just like his mother did back home, but the plant had now dried up. The other plants too didn't look as fresh as they used to be. He had watered them once on last weekend.

He knew he so much missed Kavya opening the door with a smile and running to kitchen to get some snacks and tea for him. The cupboard, the couch and the entire house that used to be so neat, clean and well-arranged was now a complete mess. He didn't want to admit, wanted to somehow suppress this feeling but then he did realise that though Kavya had left his home, but her memories left a void in his life. Earlier it was only when he was at home but now even at his workplace, she time and again came into his thoughts at times simply loosening his concentration from his work just like it happened now. It was perhaps because living with a person for over a year under the same roof, a relation that is friendly (he insisted on this word friendly to himself) and getting to know each other closely with every passing day and when that person leaves, it's natural to feel the void. He tried to explain himself and control his heart that was getting restless. He couldn't share this feeling to Jia else she would take it all in different way. She would straight away say that he had fallen for her to which he knew there wasn't any truth. Assuring and then again reassuring to himself that now he won't let himself bugged with Kavya's thoughts and memories, he got back to his cubicle for work.

Karan opened the door of his apartment and wrapping his hand around Jia's waist, pulling her close to him, he brought her inside.

"It feels so good whenever you are here at my place. I feel I am bringing home the lady of this house who needed be here, take care of this house, take care of me and take command of everything else. I so hopelessly wait for the divorce to be finalised." Karan said grabbing Jia's face into his palms and looking affectionately deep into her eyes.

"I am too waiting my love, desperately for the world to know Jia is Karan's better half; his legally wedded wife. You know, how difficult it was for me when you got married to that girl and then lived with her in this house which I had always considered mine. I felt like being disowned of all my dearest things. Every single day, thinking of you being with her under the same roof and then all the known ones calling her your wife, was something unbearable for me," Jia looked disappointed and clearly hurt while expressing her heart.

"Let's forget and bury that phase of our lives. That's not worth remembering or even giving a thought. Let's think of the future where there would be just you, me and our love. We have waited so long to be together forever and that's going to happen."

"The very first thing that I would be doing is to change the entire décor of this house. I just hate to see anything that has that girl's taste or memory attached to it. These curtains, those plants, the lights- everything!"

Listening to Jia mention the stuffs that Kavya had added to this home simply pulled him to Kavya's memories as her face suddenly reeled before his eyes. He rebuked his heart for once again disturbing him with her thoughts and forcefully pushed away her face and any random thoughts related to her. "Sure baby, do whatever you like. This is your home."

"But you know, I somehow feel your maid doesn't like me. I have marked her expressions whenever she saw me here last couple of times. She wasn't like this earlier but then in this last one year, she has changed. All I can think is Kavya's effect. I would have been branded as an 'other woman', a 'home wrecker' and don't know what else; that's how the ladies talk."

"Come on, forget it. We would change the maid. Anything you don't like would be immediately replaced. That's how my love for you is." Karan smiled bringing his face close to Jia and they allowed their lips to brush against each other. Soon they were on a long smooch and separated only when Karan's phone got ringing. It was a call from Parul.

"It was quite a long conversation with your sister!" Jia asked seeing Karan free of the call.

"Yeah, she is enjoying her married life in Singapore. She and her husband have just returned from a weeklong trip to London. She was talking about all that."

"Just that! I thought she was also advocating for Kavya and trying to convince you to reconsider your decision. Isn't it? I understand your sister has a great liking for that girl." Jia asked with a raised eyebrow not looking amused.

"How is that going to matter? I know what I have to do, and nobody can change my decision." Karan was firm, rigid and grave as he spoke out those words.

"Okay, okay lighten your mood now. I am going to get coffee for both of us." Jia walked towards the kitchen.

"Jia, I feel like having a cup of ginger tea."

"Ginger tea?" Jia stopped and turned around looking at him surprised. When did you get into this habit of having ginger tea? Now, don't tell me it was she who got you into this."

Karan suddenly realised and repented on what he just spoke out. He felt like slapping himself hard for again not coming out of anything even remotely related to Kavya. "I had this yesterday along with my colleagues in a nearby dhaba to my office. It was simply awesome." He tried to do the damage control.

"I can make that for you if you want."

"No, no. Leave it let's have coffee." Karan felt irritated with himself. The more he was thinking of getting rid of the name Kavya, more and more he felt like getting trapped into it. Brushing aside all those, he followed Jia into the kitchen to be with her while brewing coffee.

Just then Jia received a call from her mother and she walked out in the living while talking on phone. Karan took over the cup and the spoon to beat the coffee making it smooth, thick, creamy and foamy-that's how Jia liked it.

Jia came running in excitement. "Karan, there's a big news. Papa has won the election. Just now the result has been declared."

"Wow! that's a superb news. It was expected anyways. This calls for a celebration!"

"Of course, today's night would be a champagne night for us. Tomorrow after office, I plan to leave for Chandigarh for almost a week. I will talk to my boss for leave tomorrow."

"Come back soon. I will miss you and you know it's always difficult for me without you." Karan said holding her tight, close to his chest.

"Definitely, sweetheart. For me, your arms are the most peaceful place in the whole world. I will be back soon."

They cuddled up on the couch with their cup of coffee and kept kissing, caressing and hugging each other.

CHAPTER 18

Yogesh Arora glanced at his daughter who sat grim, lost and disheartened. Pulling her out of her thoughts, he addressed his daughter, "Jia, I guess your mother has already informed you why we wanted to meet you. Daughter, it could be difficult for you. You and Karan have been together since college days, love each other, want to spend life together but believe me everything that looks rosy doesn't have that goody- goody façade forever. I had agreed for him all because of you Jia but then I had always felt he wasn't a perfect match for you. I got to know from your mother that his wife had got pregnant and he didn't let you know that he had physical relation with that girl till she got pregnant. Isn't it?"

Jia looked up to her mother who had always been a friend to her and with whom she freely shared many of her personal matters. Her mother never passed on any of those to her father, but she might have thought this a matter of concern when it came to her daughter's future that she discussed it with her father. Jia's mother just nodded to her daughter's questioning eyes.

"Yes." Jia replied to her father.

"And you believed him whatever explanations he gave you. So, whenever he would be drunk, he would find you in any woman he crosses by. Isn't it ridiculous? This guy, I always knew is weak mentally, emotionally, when it comes to taking a stand or even fighting back in tough circumstances. Getting passed out from IIT and doing a government job has nothing to do with the stands you take in your personal life. Not every person who is successful in his professional life is having a great personal life too. He couldn't revolt against a marriage that was forced on him. A marriage at gunpoint is a crime and even after marriage he couldn't take a stand against it. He is a coward; he just kept thinking that those people could harm him or his family. That time too you were nowhere on his list of priorities. Once again, his family would be everything to him. Jia, our cultures, our lifestyles, the way you have been brought up, the way we all think and act - all are different. Just think when you are married to him and if ever any problem crops up between you and his family which I really see happening in future, I am damn sure he would fail to stand up to you." Mr. Arora's words sounded strong, forceful and hard hitting on Jia's mind.

After being mute for a while, she said, "Papa, he is divorcing Kavya just for me."

"Yes, why would he not do? The girl is supporting him, and her family is also not creating any ruckus. Poor girl! I am sure she has fallen for him and ready to do anything for him. And then you are beautiful, rich, command respect in society and are gullible enough so that he can convince you to believe him for anything. What else would he want? But then I know you well; you have my genes and you too are ambitious like me. And I was the same as you during my twenties a bit of an emotional fool but soon gathered senses to fly high, build up a strong business, money and now the political power too. You are my only daughter Jia and it's time for you to quit the job and that place, join our business and then later start making your way into politics. I am expecting a portfolio to be allotted to me in the government. You know, the personal life of a politician is always under scanner and I don't want people to point finger at me saying his daughter is a home breaker; yeah, that's what they would say ignoring every other fact. They just need an opportunity to dirty your linen. Earlier situation was different but now things have changed." Mr. Arora took a pause to keenly observe his daughter's facial expressions that had changed from being doubtful and disturbed to being grave and contemplating. He knew his words were making an impact on her. He continued, "Samar is a nice boy, a successful businessman and the son of Vishal Kalra, a known and strong leader of the party and a close aid to the party high command. And above all these, he has openly expressed his love for you and want to settle down with you. Jia, I don't have to say anything further. You must think, decide and act wisely. That's all!" Mr. Arora turned to his wife, they both got up and moved out of the room, for a while glancing at their daughter who seemed to be deeply engrossed into herself. Mr. Arora had strong faith in his daughter or rather his genes that wouldn't turn her into an emotional wreck and would exercise brain instead of heart.

"What the hell? Why isn't she picking up my phone?" Losing his temper, Karan muttered to himself and kicked the pot carrying the indoor plant as it tumbled on the floor. He almost threw away his cell phone on the couch and sat down with a thud. She was to be back in a week's time. Its more than two weeks now and there is no news of her. She neither picked up the phone nor replied to messages. A couple of times she disconnected his call. He had also tried on her mother's number but that too wasn't received. The last message Jia sent was - "A bit busy at home". And it was that's it. Karan simply failed to understand why she was behaving so weird. Just then, there was a beep on his mobile.

Karan almost jumped with joy as he saw the pop up- it was a message from Jia.

It read - "Karan, I want to end our relationship. I thought a lot over it and realised that I don't fit into your world. We had been together for years and that was indeed a beautiful time, but I think our paths are different. The sooner we realise the better. I have quit my job and will settle in Chandigarh. Also, I am getting married next month. So, let's end up everything here itself."

For a moment, Karan was almost numb to read the text but then his heart said it was a joke.

"Is it a joke?" He texted back.

"No, I am serious. Let's accept this truth and move on in our lives." There came an instant reply.

Karan felt as though he would faint and collapse on the floor. Never in the rarest of his dreams he had thought that Jia could do this and that too at this stage when he was divorcing Kavya to be with the love of his life and when barely a few days ago they had been together dreaming of their conjugal life as a husband and wife. "I want to talk to you now." He texted with a sinking heart and trembling fingers. But without waiting for her reply, he called her up and the phone was disconnected.

Instead he received a message from Jia, "Please don't call. There is no point talking. My reply and the reason remain the same."

Karan called her repeatedly, but phone wasn't picked up and later it was switched off.

CHAPTER 19

Sumoy looked around the mess that the home had turned into - pile of clothes here and there, uncleaned plates stinking on the table, some old newspapers gathering dust lying beneath the couch and beer bottles piled up in the terrace.

"Karan, what is all this? What have you done to yourself? You have been drinking every day," Sumoy asked concerned for Karan who seemed to have not shaved for many days, was still in his formal wear, tie loosened, half of the shirt hanging out of the pant and half of the bottle of bear already emptied by him. "So, this is what you do after being back from the office." Sumoy glanced at the glass and the beer kept on the table.

Maya who stood shocked to see their friend in such a dishevelled state, said disappointed, "Karan you are nothing but ruining yourself."

"It's nothing as such Maya." Karan led them to the couch and uncluttered it to make space for them.

"Then what is this mess you have done to your life? Can you explain? Isn't there a life beyond Jia?"

"There is and that's why I am alive."

"Good to hear that. But you need to move on now and get back to the normal life," Sumoy said holding Karan by his shoulders and trying to bring his friend out of the state he was into.

Looking at Karan, Maya said thoughtfully, "But I never expected Jia to do this. It is because of her that you are divorcing Kavya and now out of nowhere she broke up and then is all set to marry someone else. Everything was done in a jiffy. I had called her, but she wasn't willing to talk much on this. I seriously fail to understand her."

"Her Instagram post says she is engaged to some Samar Kalra and they would be heading to Turkey for a destination wedding. And you know who Samar Kalra is?" Karan said with a faded smile that had a hidden painful sarcasm.

"Who?" Sumoy asked curiously while Maya too looked on eager to know.

"He is a rich cloth merchant having his stores almost everywhere in India and the son of the newly appointed Deputy CM of the state. And now, you all know her dad too is an MLA. This explains all." Karan informed them.

"I think she would have been pressurised by her family for this alliance may be because of all the political benefits." Sumoy expressed a probability.

"I don't think so. As far as I know Jia, she isn't a girl who would buckle under anybody's pressure be it her father or anybody else. She can't be forced to do anything till she herself wishes to. I think probably she was right while saying she didn't fit into my world. After all my world is so different from theirs," Karan looked steep down on the floor as his eyes were flooded with tears which he tried to hold back.

Maya and Sumoy looked at each other shocked and disheartened to think of Jia ever doing this. "All I can say is Jia ditched you because of her own vested interest giving love and emotions a backseat. Karan it's never too late. Stop this divorce and bring back Kavya. Kavya and you are perfectly made for each other. And man, she loves you so much; you know that right. Karan, lucky are those who get true love in this selfish world and you are one of those fortunate ones. You people should be together and start life afresh," Maya suggested the best that she could think of for their friend.

"Kavya is a girl with a divine heart and I admit no one can love me as Kavya does. But I really don't deserve her. I have always hurt her feelings, never given the happiness she deserved; in fact, I never really regarded her as my wife. She cared for me, respected me and my feelings for Jia, even gave up to my physical desires and then aborted the pregnancy all for my sake. Who does all these? She is an angel in this self-centred world and deserves a much better life partner; certainly not me."

"Holy God! Is this true Karan? You never told us. She got pregnant?" Maya's eyes almost popped out to hear this revelation.

"Yes, that's true. I am a real jerk and now, I feel karma coming back to me." Karan's eyes were loaded with regret mixed pain.

"Hey, come on Karan, it's nothing like that. And I still remember Kavya telling me that you are a real generous man who cares for her and she hadn't met a man at least in her family who regarded women the way you do. We know you friend. So, don't think of karma and all. And yes, there is something Sumoy and me feel and wanted to tell you. I think you have a feeling for Kavya. If Jia ever told you this; she too would have felt. We are all humans and feelings could take a shift with time. Maybe, you never realised it and you getting close to Kavya physically could be an outcome of the feelings you had for her suppressed inside." Maya tried to explain.

Karan was silent for a moment and then said, "Tomorrow I am going to Chandigarh to meet Jia before she leaves for Turkey for her destination wedding."

"Again, back to the same. But why? You think you can change her mind in the last moment?" Sumoy didn't look amused with his decision.

"No. Just want to meet her one last time."

"Okay, we won't say anything more; just that get back to your life. A break up could be heart shattering but never an end." Sumoy's hand went out to Karan's shoulder with all the concerns for his buddy. Karan nodded, his eyes affirming it would be fine.

While driving Karan had already glanced couple of times at the bouquet of fresh flowers kept on the seat of the car and every time, he glanced at them, a smile played on his lips visualising the face that reeled before his eyes. His own decision to visit Kavya today had surprised him. He was supposed to go to Chandigarh today to meet Jia perhaps one last time or even with a remote hope of changing her mind. Though he wasn't sure about the later one if he really wanted but he did want to meet her once for all. Today he was adamant like a child who had wished for something till yesterday but suddenly he realised he would be merrier if got something else.

Karan glanced over his phone which was ringing. It was a call from Sumoy.

"Did you meet Jia? What happened?" Sumoy asked the moment Karan picked up the phone.

"I didn't go to Chandigarh." Karan replied calmly but accentuating Sumoy's eagerness.

"You did right. Thank God. I was just hoping that there wasn't a scene created at Jia's home. You are driving. Where are you now?" Sumoy asked on the other side heaving a sigh of relief.

"Going to meet Kavya at her school. I remembered, it was her birthday today and felt strongly like meeting her." Karan's voice had a sparkle which had been missing for quite some days and Sumoy could notice that well.

"Fantastic! This is one decision I am sure you will always cherish for life. Go and get her back buddy. She is the one made for you."

"And what a superb opportunist I would be. Just because my girlfriend left me to marry someone else, I should get back to the girl whom I had ditched." Karan said point blank.

"Oh come on Karan, you shouldn't be making this so complicated. It's okay if you realised your feelings late. She is still your wife." Sumoy insisted.

"Whom I am divorcing and whom I never considered my wife. Right? As far as my feeling goes, I think I should dump it aside as it has never done any good to me. As of now, I just want to meet Kavya, greet her and spend some time with her. That's all."

"I feel it's the beginning of all the good things. Carry on." Sumoy's hopes were alive for his buddy.

Karan looked at the sprawling campus of the school which had greenery all around and amidst that was situated the brick red school building. It was six in the evening and since classes were off silence had prevailed in the campus. A bit away from the mail building were the hostels for boys and girls.

Just then a guard dressed in blue and black came to him, "Sir, whom do you want to meet?"

"Kavya ma'am, she is a Hindi teacher here and stays in the campus itself." Karan replied just hoping the guard didn't ask him anything further - who he was or how he was related to her.

The guard didn't ask any further. He had already scanned him top to bottom and seemed to be impressed by his looks. Today Karan had cared to clean shave after quite a few days and was coming straight from office taking short leave, dressed in his formals. The guard led him to the meeting room and went to the office to call Kavya and let her know about the guest.

Karan hadn't informed Kavya that he was coming to meet her; he just didn't know what to tell her on phone. Karan's thoughts kept wandering into his past, present and the unpredicted future, as he waited for Kavya. He tried to push away all those random thoughts as one thing was for sure he was feeling much relaxed and better today since the time Jia had broken up with him. Till yesterday, he was restless and perturbed thinking too much on why, how, what all went around the break up. His decision of dropping the plan of meeting Jia and rather coming down to meet Kavya made him feel he successfully cut off all those emotional strings with his past that had been bugging him for days.

Kavya came in the room only to be surprised to see him there. The guard had just told her that there was a guest for her and she had been guessing who could come to meet her. Seeing Karan, instantly a pleasant smile adorned her pretty face. Karan noticed it and was reminded of the days when he used to come home and would find the same smile on her face as she opened the door. Even an emotionally dumb fellow could read her heart and say how much she loved him. Dressed in a peach chickenkari suit with dupatta spread out on right shoulder, Kavya looked graceful as always. To Karan's great surprise, a red dot of sindoor still sat prominent below her parted hair. The black mangalsutra still lay around her slender neck and then Karan's glance slipped to her finger which still had the ring given by his mother on his behalf (as he had refused to buy one for her). The process of divorce hadn't had any impact on her; nevertheless, she was still legally married. His heart pounded with an unknown joy seeing her still carrying on his name with her in all these pious signs of being a married woman.

"How are you?" She asked sitting beside him.

"I am good. How is it all going on here?" Karan asked looking straight on to her face.

"All good. This is my first job and it has been a wonderful experience till now."

"By the way, many many happy returns of the day!" Karan gifted her bunch of flowers which she accepted with a smile.

Karan's sudden dropping in to wish her had indeed stunned her. But the kind of warm and generous person she knew he was, this gesture from him was nothing awkward- Kavya thought to herself.

"Can we go out somewhere?" He asked.

"Yeah, sure," Kavya replied without a second thought. Her future may not be with him but at least whatever time God was graciously gifting her to spend with the man she loved; she certainly didn't want to miss it out.

Karan took her to one of his most frequently visited restaurants because of all the ambience and the North Indian cuisine that it was famous for. Though he had never tried to know much of Kavya's preferences, but he just guessed, she would prefer it.

They sat across the table and for a moment, they just stared at each other. Kavya looked away thinking how foolishly she was staring at him while Karan didn't intend to keep his eyes off her. For the first time he was watching her so keenly with all the interest as never before; indeed, God had used all his leisure time to make this beautiful piece of work. That's what she was- a flawless fairy with a golden heart!

"How is Jia?" Kavya broke the conversation.

This sudden question fell like a hammer on Karan's heart. He didn't want to mull over his past; that's what he took Jia now as- his past. But Kavya knew nothing that so much had changed in his life since she left. "She is fine." He replied in short not willing to talk anything more about her.

"I had talked to the lawyer couple of days back; he said there is absolutely no hurdle in our case just that it is moving on at its own pace as per the rules.

So, she had been tracking with the lawyer and was looking forward to the finalisation of the divorce. Of course, she would; after all, that's what he wanted, and it was all initiated by him. Then why wasn't he amused to hear this from her and why did her words hit him hard. Karan knew he was changing. He wasn't a fool to not understand the shift that both his mind and heart had taken.

In between, the waiter came to take the order.

"Today is madam's birthday. Can you get the best cake you have here?" Karan asked as Kavya looked at him stunned.

But then she understood, recently he had been more of a friend to her. Knowing her family wasn't here with her, he was doing all this just to cheer her up. It was such a nice gesture on his part. He certainly didn't want to end their relation on a bad note. Without saying a word, Kavya's heart just saluted him for all his good treatment and the affection he had shown to her.

Kavya cut the cake and they ordered the dinner after a while. Karan talked about her job, career ahead, her family back home and other random things. But he did avoid talking about Jia and didn't let Kavya feel in any way that Jia and he had broken up or she was getting married to someone else. All while the conversation with Kavya, he could gather that Kavya still had strong connect with his sister. She had more information about Parul than he. Also, his parents too talked to her time to time. All knew that this relation was ending in divorce but the emotional bonding that had grown between Kavya and his family was still intact. For the first time so badly, he felt he was such an unfortunate man who received a Kohinoor accidently and then lost it too. He didn't know whom to blame for his twisted fate that had heavily twisted his life too.

CHAPTER 20

Standing near the window of his bedroom, Karan glanced at the drizzle outside amidst the sunshine. It seemed as if a war was going on between sun and the rain as to who was going to overshadow whom and in this tug of war, the weather had grown pleasant bringing the greenery and shine back to the plants inside the society. Looking down from his sixth-floor apartment, he could see some kids dancing out in the drizzle. Looking around, the green climbers seemed to be sexually entwined around the white painted boundary walls and the Ashoka trees alongside the wall seemed to be hiding their affair from the world. Karan couldn't help but smile thinking of his imagination. For the last few months, he had grown a new interest in nature and his imaginations kept him engrossed in most of his free time when he wasn't working. Sumoy said such sudden change in interest happens when one falls in love. Karan knew what he hinted at and yes, he was true. Karan admitted to his self - he had fallen in love; all over again. And Kavya had taken over his heart, mind and senses. He had never believed in the theory of second chance at love. For him it was always Jia and he had never imagined anything beyond her. But Jia was now happily settled in her married life, was handling her father's business and could be seen in political rallies along with her husband. She actively posted pics on social media. Though Karan had stopped following her on any social media, some of the common friends at times updated him about her.

He had no interest left in Jia or her life in any way. He had removed the tattoo too which now didn't make any sense for him and had clearly moved on breaking all the emotional shackles.

Karan's lawyer had informed him yesterday that the entire procedure was complete, and the divorce would soon be decreed. But then his heart was constantly yelling – "Can all this be stopped? Can Kavya be back to my life? I so much want to be with her, give her all the love and respect she deserved. Who can love me more than her?" Karan restlessly paced in his bedroom as he fought a battle within whether to get Kavya back to his life or let her go since she deserved a better person (that's the reason he had given to his self to let the divorce be on). Parul had come down along with her husband for a vacation in India and his parents too had come to spend some time with all of them. Karan had entire family at his home; still he felt lonely.

"Tea and pakode for you bhai. That's the demand of the weather." Parul came with a tray and placed it on the table. Looking at him, she could easily guess all wasn't well with him. Though she found him lost most of the time since she had come here but today the matter seemed grim. Since morning he had confined himself to the four walls of his room, doing nothing and now his face said it all- he could break down emotionally anytime soon. Parul could no more see her brother in such condition. "Stop thinking so much. Both of you love each other and that's the bottom-line. Don't try to be an ethical guru blaming yourself for all this or for not giving her what all she deserved. You were merely a puppet in the hands of destiny; in fact, a victim to your ill fate and that certainly doesn't restrict you to be with her and start everything all over again. Go and let her know how much you love her and how eager you are to spend your whole life with her. Get your wife back bhai before it is too late!" Parul's words came out like a catalyst only to fuel Karan, take a stand to his life.

Karan eyes remained fixed on his sister for a while as her words kept hitting him again and gain. He quickly turned towards his cupboard, took out the car's keys from the drawer and ran towards the lift.

Everybody else in the house just couldn't understand what was so urgent that Karan left hurried and that too in this rainy Sunday. The drizzle by now had turned into heavy rain.

"Where are you going Karan? Have your lunch first." Karan's mother shouted looking perturbed but of no use.

"Let him go ma. Right now, nothing is more important to him than this," Parul tried to explain and calm down her mother.

"What is that so important?"

"It's Kavya. He has gone to get her back." This simple reply from Parul was enough to relax and bring a sigh of relief to everybody. "I had heard that good marriages begin with tears; seeing this now."

It was raining heavily wetting Karan head to toe. He wanted to meet Kavya outside the campus under the sky without any imposed rules and regulations or restrictions by the school authority. He called and informed her on phone that he waited outside.

Minutes later, Karan saw Kavya coming dressed in a simple off-white suit, holding an umbrella trying to protect herself from the rain though the heavily pouring rain and the strong wind were making it difficult for her to hold it straight. Seeing Karan on the other side of the road, she crossed it and came straight to him.

"Why are you standing here in the rain? Let's go inside." Kavya suggested looking concerned.

There wasn't any reply from Karan, but his eyes were glued to her and his heart wanted to express so much, but his lips did not move. Kavya could notice the changing colours of his face and the dilemma his heart was caught into.

"Karan, what happened? Do you want to say something?" She asked trying to put him at ease. She had to speak a bit louder to make her voice audible amidst the sound of the rain.

Karan came closer, his eyes locked into her, ready to immerse himself into those beautiful pair of eyes. They could feel the warmth of each other's breath and the pounding heart inside. "Kavya…" He muttered as the droplets of rain trickled down his nose resting on his parted lips that had a lot to say. "Kavya, come back into my life. I really need you. Even though you left, it was always you in my mind and I couldn't realise when you descended into my heart and became my lifeline. I don't know whether you are aware or not. Jia…"

Kavya interrupted looking at him with an affectionate smile, "I know everything. You are a nice man, a true gentleman and the one whom I love from the core of my heart- that's what I know and there is nothing more I am interested in." Kavya paused for a while and said further in a bit emotionally choked voice, "Life with you is wonderful."

"And without you, it's unimaginable now." Karan grabbed her tight with both his arms, his lips went on to rest on hers and those two pairs of lips could barely resist the temptation of caressing each other. A soulful love blossomed under the pouring sky.